THE IMP AT THE ICE RINK

A SOUL SEEKER COZY MYSTERY #10

COURTNEY MCFARLIN

Copyright © 2023 by Courtney McFarlin

All rights reserved.

No part of this book may be reproduced in any form or by any electronic or mechanical means, including information storage and retrieval systems, without written permission from the author, except for the use of brief quotations in a book review.

This is a work of fiction. Names, characters, places and incidents either are products of the author's imagination or are used fictitiously. Any resemblance to actual events or locales or persons, living or dead, is entirely coincidental.

1

The smell of Mediterranean food wafted toward me as Zane Matthews walked onto my porch. I think it says a lot about my power of self-control that I kissed him on the cheek before grabbing the bag and heading indoors. It's probably best that I don't mention how close I was to just grabbing the bag.

"Hey, watch it. You nearly trampled my tail."

"Sorry, Bernie. If you'd let me know you were standing directly behind me, I probably wouldn't trip over you so much. I am serious about buying you a fancy collar with a bell if you keep it up."

"What's he complaining about now?" Zane asked, watching our byplay with a grin.

"Attempted murder," Bernie said, grumbling.

I shot him a look before heading to the kitchen, looking over my shoulder to answer Zane.

"I nearly stepped on his tail, and I am a cruel, murderous woman."

"Well, we're going to disagree about that. The Brynn I know is a saint," Zane said, leaning forward to kiss the end of my nose before grabbing plates out of the cupboard behind me.

That's me, by the way. I'm Brynn Sullivan, the proud owner-slash-slave to my talking cat who's more than a cat, Bernie. Yeah, the whole talking cat thing took a while to get used to, but now I couldn't imagine not having my adorably grumpy mini-panther voicing his opinion on everything under the sun.

"Ooo, what's this?"

I dug my hand into the bag and came out with a box that was definitely not my usual Greek salad. I sniffed and closed my eyes as the scent of cumin tickled my nose.

"They have some falafel wraps I thought we'd like to try. Don't worry, I still have your salad at the bottom. And the onion rings you love so much."

"You're a prince among men."

We're definitely food-oriented people. I got everything plated and just barely kept myself from diving face-first into the wrap sitting on my plate. Zane helped me carry everything to the kitchen table, and we got settled before tearing into our food. Bernie hopped on the table, sniffing at the wrap in my hand.

"That smells good."

"I don't know if you can have falafels," I said, crunching on an onion ring. "I don't think they're good for cats. And before you say you're not a normal cat, I know. But until I know what you are, I've decided that all human treats are off the menu. I can't risk your health."

Zane smothered a laugh as an indignant look crossed Bernie's face, lighting his vibrant green eyes with anger. His furry chest swelled as he narrowed his eyes.

"That's not fair."

I took another giant bite of the wrap, which was definitely a win and going on our normal rotation of takeout food, and shrugged.

"Life's not fair. Charles said the word 'guardian,' and he meant you. What did he mean?"

Bernie turned on his tiny black feet and jumped down from the table, stalking toward the living room.

"I'm guessing he didn't answer you?"

"And you'd be correct. One of these days, I'm going to get the answers I want out of that cat. Until then, no human food. I mean it."

The eyebrow Zane raised told me he wasn't putting much stock in my ability to resist Bernie's charms. He was right, but I was going to put on a good front for as long as I could. He rolled up the wrapper for his food and leaned back, sighing.

"That was amazing. What did you think?"

My mouth was full, so I gave him a big thumbs up and nodded until I'd swallowed.

"How was your day? You said you were meeting with a new client?"

Zane ran his own security business out of the nearby town of Creekside. We'd talked about him moving in with me, and we were still in the phases of getting all of his stuff to my house in Gilded City, South Dakota.

"The guy was super nice. They want a smart home system installed in the new home they're building, with nanny cams for the kids' rooms. It shouldn't be too tough, not like Michael's house."

I grimaced and squinched my eyes shut. We were working on that project together, and thankfully, my part was almost done. Michael Chatwood was not the nicest client I'd ever had in my interior design business. On the plus side, I'd been able to help several ghosts pass on to the other side, so I was calling it a win.

"Why do they want nanny cams?"

I grabbed my plate and his and headed for the kitchen to clean up our mess. Luckily, that meant just rinsing off our plates and tossing the food containers in the recycling bag. I knew there was a reason I didn't enjoy cooking. Zane followed me and held open the bag so I could stuff all the containers in.

"I guess one of their kids is a little daredevil and they want to monitor him. They think they've got a future rock climber on their hands."

"Well, if they do, they live in the right place."

Our area of South Dakota was right in the center of the Black Hills, near the historic town of Deadwood. Cliffs were everywhere, and the rock climbing scene was getting hotter as more people discovered the area. Hanging from a rock by my fingertips wasn't really my thing, but I admired the people who did it.

"Is Logan ready to work on the house for the Millers?"

I turned on the dishwasher and leaned against it, shaking my head. I'd purchased a tiny fixer-upper in Coppertown for a couple I'd run into on one of my cases. They'd spent their lives in service to a rich family, only to be thrown out when they were entering their golden years. I'd gotten the house for a song, and my cousin, Logan, was going to help me with the renovations.

"I think so, but he's so scattered. I'm so happy for him and Kelsie, but he's been firmly in the clouds ever since they got engaged. Anyway, he's done with the Chatwood project, and I'm next on the list. This time of year, there aren't many building projects going on, so I hope nothing else has come up."

Logan took over the family construction business, and if it wasn't the dead of winter, I knew there'd be no chance he'd have time to help me. The price of the house had been covered by the reward check I'd received from the Graff estate, but everything else would come out of our pockets.

"He'll pull out of it. How are your folks?"

I levered myself off the dishwasher and walked closer, burying my head in his chest as he wrapped his arms around me. My parents met Zane during their visit over the Christmas holidays and, to my relief, they'd fallen in love with him. I stepped back so I could look into his ice-blue eyes.

"The last time I talked to my mom, she was grateful to be back in Arizona and out of the cold weather. I miss them, though. It's funny; before they came back for their visit, I knew they were miles and miles away, but I didn't miss them like I do now."

"Maybe we can take a brief trip down to visit them once we're done with the Miller house. And yes, I'm helping. This new job won't be starting until spring. It's been so cold they haven't been able to break ground on their lot. Until then, they just need to pick what they want to use."

THE IMP AT THE ICE RINK

I led Zane into the living room, where Bernie was curled up in my favorite spot on the couch. He cracked an emerald eye in my direction and closed it, wrapping his tail firmly over his face. I sat next to him and stroked his back while Zane cuddled beside me.

"I'm not starving you, bud. Besides, all you have to do is let me in on your secret, and the treats will flow again."

Silence. I sighed and shook my head while Zane chuckled. He flipped on the television, and I leaned back into his arms, zoning out into a food coma. My phone blared from the kitchen table.

"Ugh. Dang it. I should've brought it over here. I didn't think anyone would call this late."

"I'll get it."

Zane sprang up and handed me the phone before it stopped ringing. I spotted the name on the screen as I hit accept.

"What's up, Logan?"

My cousin's voice sounded like it was coming through a tin can rattling in a hurricane. Snatches of music in the background were deafening.

"Let me guess. You and your security stud are snuggled on the couch after eating an enormous meal, hibernating like a couple of bears."

While his comment stung, it wasn't far from the truth. I bit my lip and laughed.

"Maybe. Where are you? It sounds lively."

"Geez, Brynnie. You're not even thirty yet, and you act like you're in your sixties. Lively? Anyway, Kels and I are down at the ice skating rink. Do you want to join us? We're planning on hitting up your favorite restaurant afterward."

"Oh yeah, I'd heard that it was opening. Is it pretty cool?"

"It's so much fun. I haven't skated in years. Kelsie asked me to call you so you wouldn't miss out on it. They're having an eighties night, and the music is lit."

I rolled my eyes at my cousin's attempt to be hip. He was five months older than me, a fact he never let me forget, so the old age jokes weren't cutting it.

"It's pretty cold, but I'll ask Zane. We'll meet you down there if we decide to go."

"Come on, Carrot Top. You need to get out more."

I snarled through the phone as he uttered my least favorite nickname. My flame-red hair had been the source of much teasing through the years, and my cousin's method of diffusing it was to come up with increasingly absurd nicknames that made me laugh. All except that one.

"Not helping your case."

He blew a raspberry through the phone.

"Come on, it will be fun. They've got heaters and everything."

I glanced over at Zane, and he nodded, his eyes sparkling.

"Okay, we'll be there in a few minutes."

"Later, alligator."

I rolled my eyes again and stuck my phone in my jeans pocket.

"Are you sure you want to brave the cold?" I asked Zane, kind of hoping he'd want to stay home.

"Let's do it. It sounds like fun. Besides, you can corner your cousin and make sure he's going to show up tomorrow for the remodel."

"True story. Bernie, do you want to come with?"

Bernie cracked his eye open again and leveled a glare in my direction.

"Have you ever heard of a cat who enjoyed ice skating?"

"No, I can't say I have."

"There's a reason. Leave your poor, starving cat behind to fend for himself. I'll be fine."

I know it was all to get me to cave, but my heart twinged just the same. I leaned forward to give his forehead a kiss before standing.

"I hope I still remember how to skate."

Zane was holding my winter coat up for me as I walked into the kitchen. He looked as excited as a little kid, and my desire to stay home melted away. I slid my arms in and spun around.

"I'll catch you if you fall," he said, his voice husky. "I love skating. I can't wait to share it with you."

Well, shoot. When he put it like that... I shoved my hands into my gloves and felt excitement zip through my chest. Sometimes the best plans were the ones you didn't expect.

"All right, but I'm probably going to lean on you the whole time. You know how coordinated I am. I wonder if they have hot chocolate?"

"That's my girl. I'll make sure you get a giant one with plenty of whipped cream on top."

He took my hand, and we headed out into the cold. The icy blast of wind didn't faze me as I got into his Jeep, warmed by the look I saw on his face.

2

My first stop was the booth selling hot chocolate. I stood in line, bundled to my nose with my hands jammed in my pockets, and scanned the sizable crowd for my cousin. I spotted Kelsie first and waved. She grinned and walked toward us.

"Hey! You came after all. Logan said he wasn't sure."

"Shows you what he knows," I said, grumbling under my breath. "Do you want a hot chocolate?"

Kelsie's pretty face squinched up, and she shook her head.

"I'd better not. I want to make sure I fit into my wedding dress. We've only got six months until the big day."

"You've set a date? Hooray!"

Kelsie took my arm and looked at Zane, her eyes imploring him to hold our place in line. He gave her a thumbs-up and nodded while she towed me after her to a spot that wasn't crammed with people.

"What's up, Kels? Is everything okay?"

"I wanted to wait for a better time, but the longer I thought about it, the more I realized I'd better speak up before Logan does. I know we weren't the closest growing up, but that's all behind us now," she said, finally pausing for a deep breath. "Would you be my maid of honor?"

The words spilled out of her mouth so fast it took me a couple of seconds to put it all together. Years ago, when we'd been in school, Kelsie was one of the mean girls who delighted in embarrassing me. Back then, if you'd asked me if I'd consider standing up for her, I would've laughed. Hard. Now? I nodded and smiled.

"Sure. Are you sure you want it to be me?"

The look of relief that crossed her face startled me as she gripped my arm harder.

"Oh my gosh, I'm so happy you said yes. I've been thinking about this for weeks, ever since Logan asked me to marry him. It would mean the world to me."

"As long as you have no plans to shove me into a hideous dress, I'm on board. Doesn't the maid of honor need to help with planning? I'm not the best at..."

She waved her hand as we started walking back to the line. Zane was standing at the counter placing our order, so we hung back a little.

"You don't have to do all of that stuff. We're keeping it small. Family only. The people I thought were my best friends have all fallen away through the years. To be honest, if it weren't for you and Logan, and the people I work with, I wouldn't have any friends at all. You're sure you don't mind doing it?"

"Of course I'm sure. We'll have a blast. Have you found a venue yet?"

Zane appeared, somehow balancing four cups of cocoa and what looked like a massive brownie. I helped offload two cups and handed one to Kelsie. After a second of hesitation, she took it.

"I got one for Logan. Where is he, anyway?" Zane asked.

Kelsie looked over and pointed to the ice where my cousin was skating backward. Showoff. I could skate forward, well, sort of. Attempting to skate backward typically turned into a hilarious fail. She waved her free arm around, and he grinned and turned, skating toward us.

I might spend a good portion of my time ribbing my cousin, but seeing the look on his face as he clomped over to us, still on his skates, held my tongue. He looked at Kelsie with so much love my throat caught.

"Hey, doll," he said, kissing Kelsie on the forehead. "Oh, hey, Brynn. I thought you'd still be on your couch, lost in a food coma."

And the goodwill I was feeling evaporated, just like that. Funny how that works.

"I just asked Brynn to be my maid of honor, and she said yes," Kelsie said, giving a little hop. "I'm so happy."

Logan's face bunched together, and he stomped a foot.

"Watch that blade. Are you supposed to wear those outside of the rink?" I asked.

"Worrywart," he said, flicking the end of my nose. "I didn't stomp that hard. But I was going to ask you to be my best man. Well, best woman. You're my closest friend, even if you're a giant pain. Now, what am I going to do?"

I cleared my throat and aimed my head toward Zane. While the two of them had a rocky start when we first started dating, they'd become closer over the past few months. Zane held up his hand, which was still wrapped around the brownie, and shrugged.

"You don't have to do that."

"No, she's got a great idea. For once," Logan said, turning to stick his tongue out at me. "It would either be you or someone from the construction crew. May as well be you."

He softened his words with a quick punch to Zane's shoulder.

"We'll stand up for both of you," I said, linking my free arm through Kelsie's. "It will be an extra special wedding."

Her face shone as she looked between the three of us, and she nodded.

"I love it. Well, that's all settled. How about we get some skating in? I need to work off the calories from this hot chocolate."

She tossed her cup in the bin and headed toward the rink. Logan grinned over his shoulder before following her. I turned to Zane and raised an eyebrow.

"What do you have there?"

"Oh, this? Well, skating is pretty hard work, and my favorite girl might need a little sustenance later. They didn't have many left, and I know how much you love brownies..."

"Have I ever told you how much I love you?"

I snagged the brownie and put it in my inner coat pocket before draining the last of my cocoa. Zane chuckled and shook his head before following suit.

"Ready to be blown away by my ice skating skills?"

"I was born ready. Let's do this."

We walked over to the booth and got our skates sorted out. Kids crowded around the entrance to the rink, and we waited for our turn to be let onto the ice. Deadwood's newest attraction was certainly a hit with the younger crowd. I looked around the square that they'd installed and gave an approving nod.

"This is pretty cool. Did I hear it's not real ice?"

"Yep. It's some sort of special surface. I think they got the idea from a company in Europe. I'm not sure what it is exactly, but they'll be able to keep it up all winter, even if it gets warmer than usual."

I huddled into my coat as a gust of wind whipped through the square. Warm weather wasn't a big concern right at the moment. The knot of children made it onto the ice, and suddenly it was our turn. I stepped a tentative foot onto the surface and quick-stepped forward, trying to find my balance.

Zane took a giant step and spun around like a total pro while I spread my arms wide to keep from tipping over.

"This is so fun," he said, cheeks reddened with excitement. "Here, take my hand. I'll show you a few tricks."

"You're good at that."

I dropped a wink at him as I slipped my hand into his. He squeezed it and winked back before slowly leading me onto the ice.

"Look at me, not the ice. That's right. Don't look down."

I focused on his beautiful blue eyes, and before I knew it, I was gliding along gracefully. Okay, maybe "graceful" wasn't the right word, but I was certainly doing better than I thought I would.

"This is fun!"

"Watch your form. Don't lean too far back."

Zane took his hand away slowly and pressed it into the small of my back. I faltered for a second and looked down. A wisp of something skittered under my feet, and I pulled up.

"What was that?"

"What? Were you about to fall? I've got you."

"No, I thought I saw something."

I leaned forward slightly and peered into the surface below. It was remarkably like ice, but whatever I'd seen wasn't there. I shook my head and shrugged. Zane took my hand again and gently tugged me closer. I felt myself glide and laughed with delight as he kissed me on the tip of my nose.

"There's my girl. Don't get distracted. Just keep looking at me, and let's go around the rink."

I skated forward and took a deep breath. This was easier than I thought it would be. A group of kids breezed past, and I faltered, nearly tipping back. I smiled at Zane.

"I know. Don't lean back. Got any more tips? So far, I'm doing better than I ever have."

"No sudden moves. Think about each step before you take it."

Wise advice. I slowly made my way forward, and before I knew it, we were all the way around. Zane looked up as Logan and Kelsie circled past. They were laughing, lost in their own little world.

"She's good for him. I never thought he'd find the one, but I'm so glad it's her."

"Are you surprised she asked you to be her maid of honor?"

I nodded and looked down as something caught my eye again. I tugged on Zane's sleeve to get him to stop. I bent down, nearly ending up on my keister, and tried to find my balance to get a closer look.

"I saw it again. I wonder if it's a trick of the light?"

Screams cut through the laughter, and I stood, my feet flying out from underneath me. My stomach flipped before Zane's powerful arms caught me.

"Slow. I've got you. Put one foot down and then the other."

I followed his instructions and peeked around his wide shoulders.

"Over there. Something's going on."

He nodded and led me to the crowd gathered on the ice. Logan and Kelsie joined us.

"What was that? Is everyone okay?"

Two people wearing green staff vests skated past, easing people aside.

"Let us through, please."

Zane pulled me back by my coat collar and stopped me from going any further.

"You're tall. Can you see what's happening?"

Zane stood tall on his skates and leaned over, peering around the crowd.

"I see some blood. Someone must have fallen."

A guttural laugh cut through his words, and I swayed as a feeling of intense hatred swept across the ice. Pain flared in my shoulder, making me gasp.

"What was that?"

Kelsie and Logan looked at each other before looking at me.

"What? Zane just said someone might be hurt."

I shook my head.

"No, I meant that laugh. Didn't you hear that?"

"You okay, champ? Did the cold get to your brain?" Logan asked, gently knocking on the top of my beanie.

"I heard nothing," Zane said, leaning closer as he looked into my face. "You've gone all pale. Are you okay?"

I hushed him as the two staff members skated by, supporting a young boy between them. One man had a towel held to the boy's face, while the other one looked over his shoulder at us.

"It's okay, folks. We'll need to do a little cleanup, though. We need everyone off the ice for a few minutes."

Groans went through the crowd, but everyone obeyed. Zane propelled me forward, and all thoughts of having fun fled. We stepped off the ice, and I plopped down on a bench to get my skates untied.

"Brynn, didn't you hear them? It's only going to be a few minutes."

Logan mock-pouted at me, but I wasn't here for his attitude, not right now. I shook my head as I struggled with the knot of one of my laces. Zane sat next to me and put his hand over mine.

"I've got this. What did you see?"

"I don't know. There was a wisp of something on the ice. I saw it twice, and then the screams started. After that, I heard a laugh and felt this awful feeling wash over me."

He undid the knot and slid the skate off my foot.

"Give me the other one, and I'll go get your shoes. We can go home."

Logan flopped onto the bench while Kelsie looked at the ice, concern knotting her face.

"People fall on the ice all the time, Brynn. Are you sure you're not overreacting? Maybe you were allergic to something in the hot chocolate or something."

"Nice try, Logan. You know as well as I do I could marinate myself in cocoa and be perfectly fine. Something's going on here."

I quieted as the two staff members I'd seen walked by. They had their heads together, talking in hushed tones. I caught the taller man's words before they were out of range.

"That's the sixth time this week. If this keeps happening..."

I turned back to my cousin and held up my hand.

"See?"

Logan made a face, but his eyes were serious as they met mine.

"I believe you. Please don't think I don't. It's just..."

"I know. Ice skating can be dangerous. But I think there's something more to it."

I looked back at the empty rink and shuddered. The fun had been leached out of the evening, and all that was left was a vague feeling of malevolence.

"What could it be?"

Kelsie sat on the other side of me and took off her skates. Logan hopped up and grabbed them from her.

"I don't know. But I have a feeling it's just beginning."

Zane rejoined us, holding my shoes, and I slipped them on, glad to have something else to focus on. I wasn't sure what was making the hair on the back of my neck stand up, but I was determined to find out.

3

The atmosphere of our favorite Mexican restaurant was boisterous, but I couldn't shake the feeling that something terrible was going to happen. If you know me, there's not much that could make me sad when tacos were within sniffing distance, but this? This was something different.

"Brynn? Earth to freckle face…"

Kelsie elbowed my cousin in the side and, from his expression, she didn't do it gently.

"Sorry. I'm still thinking about what happened at the rink. What were you saying?"

"Now I know it's serious. And ouch, Kels. Geez, where did you learn to hit like that?"

"Brynn's shown me a thing or two. Thanks to her, I know all of your weak spots. Seriously, though. What do you think it is, Brynn?"

She turned to me, and the smile slid off her face as she searched mine. I shrugged and looked down at the menu.

"I dunno. I know I saw something. I don't think it was a trick of the light, either. I saw it twice. That poor kid got hurt, and then I heard a horrible laugh."

Zane cocked his head to the side and rubbed my back. I leaned back into his hand, luxuriating in the moment.

"What's the ice made of?"

Logan pulled out his phone and tapped on it for a few seconds before turning it around so everyone could see it.

"It's called glice. It's a polyethylene that's laminated onto sheets of plywood."

"Okay, so that clears that up. Not."

I made a face before focusing back on the menu. I didn't know what polyethylene was, but I would bet a week's worth of tacos it didn't have goofy things running through it. I closed the menu with a slap and drummed my fingers on it. I wasn't hungry, especially after our Mediterranean feast earlier, but I didn't want to sit and stare at the table while Logan and Kelsie ate.

Logan took his phone back and was nodding while he read through whatever site he was on.

"This stuff is actually amazing. When you're done with it, it can be stacked and put away until the next season. Although technically, you could skate on it all year. How cool would that be?"

"Does it say anything about the material being cloudy or having strange wisps that go through it?" Kelsie asked, shooting me an apologetic smile.

"No, nothing about that. So, you're thinking it's paranormal?"

Right as Logan asked, our server appeared. Her friendly smile slid into perplexed territory, but she shook it off and turned to Zane.

"Are you ready to order, Sugar?"

My eyes narrowed as she fawned all over Zane. Yeah, I mean, I get it. He's hotter than any man had a right to be, but times like these made me wish I could carry around a big stick. What? Not to hit people. Just to shake threateningly.

"I'll let my girlfriend order first," Zane said.

He's a champ, isn't he?

"Thanks, honey. I'll have the nachos with guacamole, please."

"I'll split that with her."

Zane handed our menus to our server and put his arm around

me. I snuggled into his side while Kelsie and Logan ordered their food. Kelsie waited until our server walked away to lean closer.

"What kind of laugh was it? Creepy? Evil?"

"Yes and yes. Honestly, the first thing that came to mind when I heard it was an evil clown."

Logan blanched and shifted in his seat.

"What? You don't like clowns?" Zane asked, his eyes lit with amusement.

"I didn't say that," Logan said, raking his hand through his hair. "You don't think it's a clown, though, right? I mean, we didn't see any clowns while we were there."

"I don't think it's a clown, but it had that vibe. You know that one horror movie with the clown that lures..."

"So, about the little house in Coppertown? I can meet you there tomorrow so we can put a plan together."

My cousin, even though he was a hard-working man's man, had one secret fear. I wouldn't blab it to everyone, but I let him change the subject.

"Sure, that sounds good to me. What time?"

"Nine? That should give you time to snuggle with Lover Boy here and peel yourself out of his arms. Oh yeah, are you two ever going to finish moving in together?"

My urge to be nice to Logan evaporated.

"So, as I was saying about that movie. You know the one, Logan? I think we watched the original when we were kids. I think they updated it recently. We should have a couple's night and watch it together."

Logan's eyes narrowed while Kelsie hid her grin behind her hand. Zane's chest vibrated with a silent laugh.

"That might be fun. As for moving in together, my landlord found someone to take over the lease. My last day is at the end of the week. Sorry, honey, I was going to surprise you, but with everything going on, it slipped my mind."

"Was it Grace? After everything that happened with the theater, I wasn't sure she was going to stay."

Zane nodded and took a sip of his soda.

"I'm pretty sure it's her."

"It is," Kelsie said. "I heard from her yesterday. She's so excited. I still can't believe how that all went down."

I rubbed my shoulder and shivered. Even though I'd been miraculously healed, I still felt the occasional twinge from where I'd been stabbed. Zane's smile slipped, and he scooted closer on the bench.

"Are you okay? The skating didn't aggravate it, did it? I didn't even think of that."

I waved off his concern.

"I'm fine. I was just thinking. When I heard the laugh, my shoulder hurt. I wonder if it's somehow connected."

"Maybe because you were healed in the spirit world, you have some lingering ghost gunk inside of you."

Once again, our server appeared at the exact wrong time. I pasted a weak smile on my face as she handed over our food. She dropped the nachos in front of Zane and left without another word.

"Well, let's hope we don't sit in her section again," I said, watching her walk away. "Those fajitas smell amazing."

"Hands off," Logan said, leaning over to smack my hand lightly. "You already ate dinner and you're having nachos. Eat those."

"Hey, don't do that."

Zane's voice was quiet, but there wasn't any way of missing the thread of steel that ran through it. Logan sat back and shook his head.

"I mean nothing by it. You know how Brynn and I are. We goof off all the time."

"I know. I don't mean that. She just said her shoulder hurt, and you smacked the hand on that arm. Geez, man. Think."

My cousin looked instantly contrite.

"Sorry, Brynnie. I didn't even think about it."

"It's fine. It doesn't hurt anymore."

An awkward silence settled over the table until Logan cracked another joke, and we dug into our food. Even though I rarely pass up food, I picked at the nachos. I could feel Zane watching me as I pushed the plate closer to him.

"I had that hot chocolate and a huge dinner. Besides, I might want to eat that brownie you got me later on."

I patted the pocket that still held the chocolate goodness. By the time Logan scarfed down his fajitas, and Kelsie finished her taco salad, leaving, of course, the best part, the shell, uneaten, I was more than ready to head home. By consensus, we'd tabled any talk of what happened on the ice rink and focused instead on talking about the house renovations.

"Is there anything I could do to help?" Kelsie asked. "I know I don't have the experience you two have, but I'd love to help. I'm a great cleaner."

I smiled, surprised by her offer.

"I'd never turn down a request to help. I thought you'd be busy with wedding planning, though."

"I'll make time. I love what you're doing for the Millers, and I'd love to help. Besides, now that I'm marrying this guy," she said, thumbing in Logan's direction, "I need to learn more about the trade. I don't want to work at the hotel for the rest of my life."

Logan's eyes gleamed as he took her hand. Kelsie continued to surprise me, and it was clear Logan appreciated the change as much as I did.

"Thanks, babe. You don't have to get dirty, though."

She snorted and waved him off.

"Maybe I want to. I've seen the magic Brynn can do with wallpaper and paint, and I'd like to learn how to improve our future home."

Logan's face clouded, and he drummed his fingers on the table.

"That's right. Now that you're getting married, you'll be moving in together. Duh. Have you found a house yet?"

Kelsie pushed her plate to the middle of the table and shook her head.

"No. I'm renting, and Logan's house is small. I mean, it's fine for right now. But if we want to have kids..."

I opened my mouth to suggest talking to Bob, but my cousin caught my eye. He shook his head slightly, and I caught the message.

"Well, I'm sure something will come up. The market's crazy right now, anyway."

"True story."

Our server came back and dropped off the check after picking up our dishes. There was a brief struggle between Zane and Logan for the check, but to my shock, Logan won. He never volunteered to pay for anything. It looked like everyone was turning over new leaves lately.

We shuffled out of the booth and headed for the parking lot while Logan paid the bill. My breath streamed out in a cloud as we waited for him to join us. Kelsie let out an eek sound, and I rolled my eyes as Logan appeared behind her, pressing his likely freezing hands to the back of her neck.

"That never gets old."

"You keep telling yourself that."

"Whatever. See you tomorrow, Freckles. Don't let the bed bugs bite."

I stuck my tongue out at his back as they walked away, and Zane chuckled.

"You two are something else."

"He started it."

He shook his head and wrapped an arm around me.

"After you meet with Logan, are you going to head to the library?"

"How do you know me so well?"

He opened the door of his Jeep for me and shot me a roguish smile.

"I know my girl."

I waited until he hopped into the driver's side and fired up the engine.

"That's the plan. I have little to go on, do I? But it's been a few weeks since I've seen Sophie, and she might have some scuttlebutt."

He held up a hand while he drove us home, ticking off a few points.

"Number one, it's in a historic square. Number two, you definitely saw and heard something weird. Three, it's happened a few times."

"Six."

"Six what?"

"It's happened six times."

"See? That's something. It may not be much, but I have faith you'll get the answers you need. You always do."

He gripped my hand as I leaned back against the headrest. He was right. Maybe the location of the rink was the most important factor. While I could spend some time researching it before bed, my eyes were heavy, and I couldn't wait to get cleaned up, snuggle with Zane, and go to bed. Oh, and maybe eat that brownie. Didn't want to forget about that.

4

I stood at my kitchen counter, blinking at Bernie as he sat at my feet. I'd spent a restless night tossing and turning and felt like something that should probably be covered up in a litter box. It might have been the brownie, but I'm always hesitant to blame baked goods for anything.

"Are you going to withhold my regular rations as well to browbeat me into revealing my true nature? Do you think starvation will get what you want?"

Sigh. Bernie was dramatic on a good day, and from where I was standing, the day hadn't started all that great. But that just meant there was room for improvement, right? I just needed to keep telling myself that.

"No, bud. I won't starve you. See? I've already got your bowl ready, and I'm just debating which food to give you."

"As if it matters."

He scuffed a coal-black paw on the floor and attempted to look pitiful by sucking in his sides. Considering he was well-fed and glossy, it didn't work. Okay, it might have worked a little.

"Salmon. Your favorite. Hey, I never got to tell you what happened last night."

I spooned up his food while I brought him up to speed on the ice rink. When we'd returned the night before, he'd been absent, and a quick search hadn't revealed his hidey-hole. I'd let him be, figuring he'd be less sulky in the morning. Ha.

"Wait. Say that again?"

"And then we went to eat Mexican food?"

"No. Not that part. You heard laughter?"

I placed his dish in front of him and stepped back.

"I thought you were starving."

The look he shot me promised retribution later. Even if he wasn't entirely a cat, he still liked to misbehave like one. I glanced at the living room couch, which bore the marks of his past tantrums, and sighed again. He tucked into his food, spraying a little as he talked.

"Laughter?"

"Yeah. I heard a hideous laugh right after the kid went down. Oh, and my shoulder hurt. What do you think that means?"

He gave a kitty shrug and went back to his meal, leaving me free to get my coffee going. On days like today, I really wondered about the whole cats-before-coffee thing. He couldn't fool me, though. Even though it looked like he was simply eating, that brain tucked under those cute little ears was working overtime.

"Hey, gorgeous. Do I smell coffee?"

Zane popped into the kitchen, rubbing his neck. He skirted the pieces of food surrounding Bernie's bowl and got his own mug, joining me in my vigil at the coffeemaker.

"Good morning. Did you sleep well?"

I winced as I asked, knowing full well my restless night had leeched some of his sleep away. He was too nice to say anything, though.

"Not bad. Did you ever fall asleep?"

"I got an hour or two after five. Here. You can have the first cup."

Did I glance longingly at the brain juice I handed Zane? Yes. Yes, I did. But it was the least I could do. I turned my attention back to the coffee pot and willed it to drip faster. We really needed one of those newfangled machines, but I was attached to this pot that I'd gotten back when I bought this house.

"Mmm. That's good. New blend?"

I opened the cupboard and grabbed the bag I'd used.

"Yeah. Mallory recommended it. It smells amazing."

"And tastes even better. Here, have a sip."

He's a prince among men. I took a sip and closed my eyes as the flavors rushed over my tongue. Yep, this brand was a keeper. And so was Zane.

"I feel human now," I said, handing the cup back. "What do you have planned for today?"

We talked through our plans while Bernie cleaned up after his meal. He swiped his paw over an ear one more time while I filled my cup.

"Describe the laughter."

I turned to him and cocked my head to the side.

"Evil clown is what I came up with last night. Why?"

"High-pitched or low?"

"Low."

"Interesting. I'm coming with you today."

I waited for him to elaborate, but he'd gone back to bathing. If I knew my cat, he wouldn't say anything else until we were on the road. I shook my head and drained my cup.

"I'd better get ready so I can get up to the house before Logan gets there. I still haven't had extra keys made."

"I'll get some made from the spare you gave me," Zane said, rinsing his cup and putting it in the dishwasher. "Tell Sophie hello for me when you see her. I'd better get ready, too. I'll need to be in Creekside all day, but tomorrow I can help with your project."

He wrapped me in a quick hug that chased away the dregs of my morning grumpiness, and we headed back to my bedroom. Or I guess it was going to be our bedroom. I paused as I watched him pull his clothes out of the dresser. I'd already ceded a few drawers for him. I'd never lived with anyone, but I had a feeling this was all going to work out.

"What?"

Zane turned and caught me staring at him. I smiled as I walked closer.

"Just thinking about how happy I am that you're moving in. I can't wait."

"I just have a few more boxes, and I'll be all set. I plan on grabbing those tonight on my way up here, if that's okay?"

"It's perfect. We'll have to have a special meal and celebrate."

"I'll even cook."

He kissed the end of my nose before heading across the hall to the bathroom. My little one-bedroom house had never been big, especially with just Bernie and me rattling around inside, but would it feel small with the addition of Zane? I shrugged and got ready for the day. Only time would tell, and I had enough on my plate already.

Before I knew it, I was strapped into my car, heading up the hill to Coppertown. Bernie sat next to me in the passenger seat, staring out at the world as it flew by.

"Has it only been children who were affected?"

I turned down the radio and looked over at my cat. He'd been silent for most of the journey.

"I'm not sure. I guess I'll have to check. I don't know how willing the rink employees will be to answer questions, though. It's brand new, and the last thing they need is bad press."

"Sophie might know. She hears a lot."

"Good point. Do you want to hang out in the car while I meet with Logan? It shouldn't take too long. I don't want you to be cold. We don't have heat in the house yet."

Bernie gave his version of an eye roll, coupled with his signature shrug.

"Oh, now you care about my well-being. You know, if you shared your breakfast, I'd have enough calories to make sure I was warm."

"I didn't have breakfast."

"Exactly. You should find a drive-through and remedy that. A breakfast sandwich would go down a treat."

"Sorry, bud, but that's not happening. My stomach is a little iffy after last night."

He mumbled something about mixing cuisines and chocolate, but I tuned him out as I focused on the street signs so I didn't miss my turn. I came to a stop in front of the tiny house and parked.

It didn't look like much, not yet, but in a few months, I couldn't wait to see what the transformation would look like. I'd beaten Logan, which meant I'd have some time to walk through the place by myself and get some much-needed inspiration.

"You're sure you want to go inside?"

"Wouldn't miss it. Let's go."

Bernie hopped out as soon as I opened my door and streaked up the hill to the house. That darn cat. I followed at a much slower pace and picked my way across the ramshackle porch. The outside work was going to wait until it thawed, but that meant we could focus on bringing out the beauty of the inside.

I opened the door, and Bernie ran ahead of me. I shivered as I shut the door. Once we were done with the demolition, the heat was going to be the first thing on the list. I walked back to my favorite room, the kitchen, and stood in the center of the floor.

"Why is it you always like kitchens, but you're a terrible cook?"

"Thanks for that. I don't know. I think it's because it's the heart of the home. And you know how much Mimi likes to cook. I can only imagine the dishes she'd come up with in here. I need to make sure it does her justice."

He sniffed and trotted out as I heard the front door open.

"Honey? I'm home."

"I'm in the kitchen, Logan."

His boots sounded like industrial clogs as he clomped into the small space. His cheeks were ruddy with the cold, and he smacked his hands together.

"Morning, Red. What's shaking? Where's that hunky security stud? I thought he was going to help."

"Zane, which is his name, as you know, had to go into Creekside.

He's going to help tomorrow. Besides, we're just doing a walkthrough today. How's Kelsie?"

"Great. We stayed at her place. That's why I'm a little late."

"Hey, speaking of that. Last night, when Kelsie brought up housing, I was going to recommend calling Bob, but you told me to shut it. What's up with that?"

"I didn't tell you to shut it. I gave you our look, but I said nothing."

"Details, shmetails. What's up?"

"Not now, Brynn. What's the plan for the kitchen?"

Wow. I was not expecting that. Even though I really wanted to pry, his tone put a quick kibosh on that. I changed gears and led him on a walkthrough of the house, room by room. Once we'd ended back up in the entryway, Logan felt more like himself, but I could tell something was off.

"I like the plan we put together. I'll be back tomorrow, and Zane's going to make sure you have some extra copies of the keys so you can come and go as you please."

Logan put his hands on his hips and nodded, looking at the ceiling.

"Fine. I need to get up into the attic. A lot of these old homes have wood rot, and I want to make sure we're covered before we insulate. This place is freezing."

I followed his eyes and nodded slowly. Structural work was the last thing I wanted to contemplate, but he had a point. We couldn't afford not to fix the framing if it had issues.

"Let's do that later. I want to get to Deadwood and talk to Sophie."

He nodded and turned to leave, his face closed off. Typically, I could read my cousin like a book. We'd been close since we could crawl, and it wasn't like him to hide anything from me. Something was definitely up with him.

"Later, Freckles."

He stomped off the porch and headed down the hill, hands shoved into his pockets. Bernie joined me, and we watched Logan get into his pickup.

"He's hiding something."

"No kidding, Sherlock. The question is: what? He was over the moon when Kelsie said yes. Do you think he's regretting popping the question?"

Bernie blinked and shook his head.

"Who knows? She's good for him, but you know Logan. It wasn't too long ago he was footloose and fancy-free."

I picked at the peeling wood on the trim before catching myself. I'd planned on refinishing as much as I could, and having a sizable gap where I'd pulled off a splinter wouldn't help.

"Well, let's head down to Deadwood. I'm starving."

"So am I."

"You know, I'd be happy to share my food with you. All you need to do is come clean."

"Then again, I'm not that hungry."

He stalked ahead of me, tail held high, while I locked the door and followed. I was feeling guilty, but I knew I had to be strong. Maybe once he smelled my food, he'd reconsider. I got in the car and cranked the heat, holding my hands up to the vents to thaw.

"You know what sounds good? A breakfast burrito."

Bernie's emerald eyes were slits as I put my car in drive and pulled out of my parking space. I gave him a cheery smile as I turned around and headed to Deadwood. Somehow, I was going to get him to come clean.

5

Despite making it known how delicious my breakfast burrito was, Bernie wouldn't budge. He turned his back to me while I ate and refused to ask. I could tell from his twitching whiskers that I was making progress. Once I'd balled the wrapper up and stuffed it into the takeout bag, he finally turned to face me.

"All done with your feast?"

His eyes were enormous in his little face, and my heart twinged. Painfully. I didn't know how long I could keep this up.

"It was okay. Ready to head to the library? I know Sophie would love to see you."

"That sounds fine."

I put the car in drive and headed down the back streets of Deadwood. The novelty of snow had long since worn off, and everything looked dreary. Spring was many months away, but there would be plenty of events to keep everyone in good spirits until the green grass poked through the ground. Until then, I had plenty on my plate.

Once I'd parked, I looked at Bernie and raised an eyebrow. I'd bent and allowed him to travel in the car without being inside his carrier, but I drew the line at letting him roam the library freely.

While I knew Sophie wouldn't mind, the patrons might, and I didn't want to upset anyone.

"Fine. I'm going."

He heaved a sigh and darted into his bag, turning around to face me while I zipped him up. I gave him a quick boop through the mesh and smiled before sliding out and carefully putting the strap on my shoulder.

"Come on, bud. Maybe we're about to learn something interesting."

"That's the only reason I'm still in this car."

"I don't think you'd enjoy walking home. That's a lot of miles for a little cat."

"Well, I can..."

He trailed off, and I could feel him shift in his bag as we got to the entrance of the library. I waited for him to finish, but someone walked out and held the door open for me, giving me a curious look. Yeah, I was standing there, staring at the door, so I get it. I nodded and walked in, ducking my head.

"Brynn! What a saving grace on this dull day."

My friend Sophie Ryman swept from behind the desk like a dervish, bracelets tinkling and her long skirt whipping around her legs. She wrapped me in a hug.

"It's good to see you, Soph. I love the blue."

Ever since Tabby Reed had entered our lives, my friend had been trying out streaks of fashion colors in her gray hair. She looked fabulous as she stepped back and ran her fingers through her hair, disturbing the streak of violet that threaded through the front.

"Are you sure? I really liked it in the tube, but I'm not sure I like it on my head."

"Well, I think it looks great. It makes me think of the first wildflowers that pop up on the mountain after the last frost."

"How poetic, dear. I like that. Oh, you brought your magnificent cat with you. Hello, Bernie. So, what are we diving into today?"

She threaded her arm through mine and led me back toward our favorite research spot, The Dakota Room. I stifled a laugh, tickled that she didn't even have to ask. She knew me that well. Sophie was in on my big secret and had been invaluable in solving more cases than I could count. Her research skills, coupled with her vast knowledge of the town and its inner workings, were world-class.

"Honestly? I'm not sure."

Her steps faltered, and she shot me a quizzical look as we entered the room. I put Bernie's bag up on the long table that ran through the center and crossed my arms over my chest. I felt vulnerable as I related what I'd experienced the night before. My friend listened patiently before tapping her finger to her lip.

"I see. Well, isn't this a fine kettle of fish? A mysterious laugh. A feeling of malevolence, and what a wonderful word that is, isn't it? People being injured, which of course is not wonderful. Well, let's put our heads together and see what we can find out."

She disappeared into the stacks, leaving me alone at the table. Bernie cleared his throat, and I looked down.

"You forgot to mention the pain in your shoulder. I think that's important."

"Oh. I'll do that later."

It didn't take Sophie long to come back, carrying a stack of books. She thumped them down and immediately started splitting them between us.

"So I pulled everything I could find on the history of the square. It's only been recently renamed. If we want to be historically accurate..."

"Which we always do..."

"It was the yard for the stage company back in the late 1800s," Sophie said, flashing me a grin.

"Really? I didn't know that."

"Few do. Did you know the original coach that was used was purchased by Buffalo Bill and used in his shows?"

"Add another I didn't know to the pile. That's fascinating."

"But it's not what we're here to learn, is it? So, let's get down to business."

"Do you need to monitor the front? I didn't see Stacia."

Sophie checked the slim watch on her wrist and wrinkled her nose.

"She'll be back from her break in a few minutes. I'll text her and let her know I'm back here if she needs anything. It's been so slow today; I don't think it will matter too much."

She took a seat across from me, and I cracked the first book, paging through a brief history of the stage company that ran in Deadwood through the gold rush. It was truly interesting, but I found nothing that seemed pertinent. Sophie heaved a sigh and closed her book.

"Not much here, is there?"

I didn't want to be a downer, so I put on a smile and shrugged.

"Not yet, anyway."

"Let's shift gears. There's a book in here that sums up the history of the town by subject. Once we know what we're looking for, we can search through the newspaper."

Bernie started moving around in his bag, and Sophie glanced over before darting to the door that separated the room from the rest of the library. She kicked the door stopper out of the way.

"I should've thought of this earlier. Let him out. I'm convinced he's smarter than both of us combined."

I might have heard Bernie agree, but I wouldn't share that information. Instead, I unzipped his bag, and he came out slowly, stretching, while Sophie cooed over him and scratched his favorite spot behind his ears.

"Look at you. You're more handsome every time I see you."

Bernie preened and tossed me a look. I rolled my eyes before grabbing a new book. It was enormous, and from the title, I had high hopes I might find something interesting inside its covers.

Bernie sat just close enough so he could see the book without actually touching me. I rolled my eyes before stroking his black fur. He gave a little hop, pushing his head into my hand, letting me know that while all may not be forgiven, we were still buds.

"Start with the index."

"But I don't know what we're looking for," I said as quietly as I could.

Sophie glanced up. Luckily, she was a fellow bookworm and tuned out voices when she was reading. Whew.

"I think I do."

I raised an eyebrow at my cat and obeyed his order, paging to the index at the back of the book. It was an older work, and the pages felt fragile as I turned them.

"Stop. Right there. Robberies. Focus on the connection with the stagecoach."

"Really? Why?"

Bernie closed his eyes in frustration at my whispered question, and I bit my tongue. The look he shot me when his eyes opened made it clear I just needed to turn to the page noted and stop talking.

I shifted in my seat and started reading. The answer to my question was right in the first paragraph. One of the most notorious robberies in the state's history was centered right around the town square. I bit my lip as I read, wishing I could absorb the book. My heart raced, and I turned to my friend.

"Sophie? Have you ever heard of an outlaw called Lame Jim?"

She closed her book and cocked her head to the side. I knew her powerful mind was sifting through centuries of information she'd gleaned over the years. Her eyes flared brightly, and she nodded.

"I do. He was part of a gang that pulled off the robbery of the gold mine's payroll. They never found all the money."

"Really? What happened to him?"

She leaned back in her chair and fiddled with her bracelets.

"It's a sad story, really. The robbery was brutal, and a few of the guards were killed. The gang actually got away with their loot, and it took ages to bring them all in. They split up, with some heading to the state's capital, Pierre, while others headed into Native land. Lame Jim was one of the latter. I believe he was the last one they found. Not one stood trial."

I sensed there was more to the story.

"What happened?"

"Back in those times, it took forever for a judge to get to the territories. Trials would be scheduled out for months, while the locals wanted justice and wanted it fast. I believe most of the gang members ended up hanged by posses. Lame Jim was the last one to be taken. He was hanged right in the square."

My stomach plummeted as the pieces came together.

"Do you think?"

"It's entirely possible you're dealing with his angry spirit. I'm not sure, though. Let's pull up the newspaper archives and see what we can find. We've got a direction to follow now!"

She hopped up and headed to the computer, tapping her fingers on the mouse while she waited for it to load. She crowed triumphantly once the screen flipped on and typed furiously. I blinked in surprise at the amount of results that came back from her search.

"Wow. That's a lot of mentions."

"It was a big moment, especially since the mine never got their money back."

She glanced at her watch and opened a bunch of tabs, printing each one as it loaded.

"Now you can take all the stories home with you. One of these days, I need to see if the library can allow access to these archives so patrons can just search from their home computers. But that would mean I wouldn't get to see your smiling face."

"I wouldn't let convenience stop me from coming to see you. Thanks so much for doing all of this."

She waved off my thanks and straightened, smoothing her skirt.

"There. They'll all be ready at the front desk. I just need to get these books put away."

"I'll help. Many hands make light work."

I stacked the books and trailed after her, helping return them to the right sections.

"Did I tell you Tabby Reed is planning to come back for another visit?" Sophie asked, grinning as she slid the last book into place.

"No, but that's wonderful. How's she doing?"

The two librarians had developed a close friendship during Tabby's time in the Black Hills, and it made my day to see how happy Sophie was.

"Great. She's still on the fence about moving back here, but I keep telling her our winters are just like the ones in Chicago. Okay, maybe we get more snow, but it's more fun here. I spent a few winters in the Windy City when I was a girl, and I'd take a South Dakota winter any day over what they have there."

"Well, if anyone can convince her to make the move, it's you. When is she coming?"

"Most likely Easter, but we'll have to see. We're planning a bunch of activities and day trips. Maybe you can come with us on some of them."

"I'd love that."

We spent the better part of another hour catching up on our lives, and before I knew it, the light coming in the window had faded as the sun dipped below the hills. Night came early in this part of the state in winter. I zipped up Bernie's carrier and followed Sophie to the front desk. Sophie ducked behind and pulled out a fat stack of printouts, handing them across to me.

Stacia was checking someone out, so I just waved as Sophie followed me to the door.

"I know I said winters aren't that terrible, but I can't wait for spring."

"That makes two of us, Sophie. But at least we can head home, cuddle under a blanket, and stay warm. Looks like I'll be doing that tonight with some of these articles."

"True. I've been thinking I need to stop by the shelter and adopt a cat. Seeing you with Bernie always makes me wish I had one. I could even bring him to the library during the day so he wouldn't be lonely. I've seen several libraries that have cats in the stacks, and I think one would be a great addition here."

Her face lit up as she talked about her plans, and warmth surged through my middle. I worried about my friend being lonely, but it sounded like she had the perfect plan.

"I'd do it! I'm sure there are plenty of kitties who could use a wonderful home, and you'd be a great cat owner."

Her bracelets jingled as she clasped her hands together.

"I'll do it tomorrow. Hopefully, the shelter will be open. If I find one, I'll let you know so you can swing by. Maybe by then I'll have found something useful for you."

"You always do. See you soon, Sophie."

"Have an enchanting, exhilarating…"

"Educational evening?"

"I love it!"

We exchanged a hug after our ritual word game, and I headed back outside, strangely hopeful. I hadn't found what I was looking for, but I was convinced the answers I was seeking were just around the corner. The still warm-from-the-printer papers in my hand may just hold the key to figuring out what was going on.

6

Once we were safely in the car, away from prying ears, I turned to my cat. It was obvious from the way he was shifting around in his carrier that he had plenty to say. He popped out as soon as I unzipped him.

"Finally."

"Are you okay? You seem restless."

"You mean, besides the fact that I'm starving? Literally wasting away in the face of your cold-heartedness."

I pursed my lips. I suppose after my performance with the breakfast burrito earlier, I kind of deserved it. His huge, pleading eyes weren't making me feel any better.

"All right, let's head home and crack a can of your favorite food."

"What else is for dinner? I could eat a horse."

"I'm not sure what Zane and I are having. Do you think it will contain a side of your origin story?"

His beautiful eyes narrowed, and he faced the front of the car. I pulled out of the parking lot and thought about everything we'd learned, remembering how he'd pointed me in the right direction.

"How'd you know we'd need to research a robbery?"

He was quiet for a second, and I focused on the road, turning onto the highway that would take us home.

He finally turned, and I'm pretty sure, underneath that black fur, he had an eyebrow raised.

"Honestly? I guessed."

"Hey!"

"Well, Sophie mentioned the area where the rink is used to be where the stage was, and I put two and two together."

"I think that's some pretty good thinking, bud. Hopefully, we'll find some information about the robbery in those printouts Sophie gave us. We'll have our work cut out for us, wading through it. I wonder if we can get Zane to help."

"I'm sure he'll be happy to assist. However, there is someone else I think we should ask."

"Who? Mallory?"

"Yes, but not exactly."

I looked over at my cat and almost missed my turn.

"What do you mean, not exactly?"

"There's someone we know who was alive back then. I think we need to pay him a visit."

It took me a second to figure out who he meant, and I immediately started shaking my head.

"No. Nope. Not gonna do it."

"Come on, Brynn. You know he's the best resource we have. Charles is wonderful, but he was in the area a little too late. We need to go to someone from back then."

"Couldn't we head up to the old graveyard and see if there's anyone else hanging around? Literally anyone else?"

He cocked his head to the side before shaking it.

"That's not a bad idea. In fact, we probably should do that. But you know as well as I do, Ned's our guy."

The problem, well, one of them, was that he was right. Edward Davis, or Ned, as he preferred to be called, was the spirit of a miner who'd been alive in Deadwood during the gold rush. He was the perfect resource. The other problem was Ned was a different ghost.

"We literally couldn't ask for anyone better," Bernie said, pressing the issue.

"We could, but I don't think their ghosts are around. At least they weren't the last time I went up to Mount Moriah."

Bernie chirped, likely remembering the time I'd dragged him up to the old cemetery when I was in high school. I'd been convinced I could talk to the ghosts of Wild Bill and Calamity Jane, but alas, they weren't around. While I was glad they'd hopefully moved on, it still would've been amazing to speak with them.

"Fine. You're right."

"As usual."

I grumbled as I pulled to a stop in front of my house. Zane was already home. A zip worked its way down my spine as I sat for a second after turning off the engine. This was different. Coming back to my little home and seeing it already lit up and welcoming, knowing the man I loved was inside. Bernie chirped and made eye contact.

"I'm glad he's around."

"That makes two of us. Ready to go in?"

He darted into his bag, and I zipped it up before getting out. The colder temperatures and the promise of a warm welcome gave my feet wings, and I made it to the door in record time. I dug in my pocket for my keys, smiling when the door opened to reveal Zane.

"Hey, beautiful," he said, leaning over to kiss my cheek.

He grabbed Bernie's bag and released the cat, bending down to pet him while I took my coat off and tossed it onto the hook by the door. The house was full of light. I could definitely get used to this. The scent of something delicious perked me up.

"How was your day? What's that incredible smell?"

"Long and lasagna."

We shared a laugh as I followed him to the kitchen, skirting the boxes he'd stacked near the kitchen table.

"That's the last of the boxes? I'll help you put everything away after supper. Something tells me that's not a frozen lasagna in the oven, either."

He dropped a wink over his shoulder before opening the oven to check on his concoction.

"Of course not. Made from scratch, using my old neighbor's recipe. Did you know that true Italian lasagna doesn't use ricotta?"

"I didn't."

Bernie swiped his tongue around his muzzle and gave me a longing look before turning the full power of his gaze onto my boyfriend. Zane caught it and shrugged.

"Bud, you know I'd love to give you a little taste. Especially since I think you'd love the béchamel sauce, but I don't want to get in between your feud with Brynn."

My forehead wrinkled into a frown.

"It's not a feud. Well, not exactly. You know what, Bernie? It's a special night and a celebration, so we'll forget about the whole no treat thing. For tonight anyway."

He skittered around the kitchen, bouncing off the cupboards in glee, and I couldn't help but giggle at his antics. I know, I know. I'm a big softie. Honestly, I couldn't believe I'd gone this long without giving in. I grabbed his bowl to dish up his actual food, even though I knew he'd prefer an enormous plate of pasta. I didn't mind spoiling him with a little treat, but he still needed his regular food. Bernie trotted over and tucked into his food, making little smacking sounds.

Zane closed the oven door and turned to the fridge.

"How does a salad sound?"

My stomach spoke for me with a tremendous growl, and I nodded, making my ponytail bounce.

"I'll take that as a yes. Do you want to put it together while I make the dressing?"

"Of course."

I started washing the lettuce and tomatoes while Zane dug through the cabinets, hunting for the ingredients he needed.

"Why was your day long?" I asked, shaking the water off the lettuce and putting it aside.

"It was just one of those days where everything goes a little wrong. Nothing bad happened, but it was just a little frustrating. How was the house? Your cousin? Sophie?"

I held up my fingers, ticking off my answers.

"Great, but we're going to need to get heat there soon if we're going to work inside. Logan's okay. I think there's something going on with him, though. Do you think he's regretting proposing to Kelsie? Sophie's a champ. I swear she knows more about Deadwood's history than anyone else."

Zane blinked at my rapid-fire answers before turning back to his dressing.

"What's wrong with Logan?"

I started ripping the lettuce into smaller pieces as I brought up Logan's strange behavior when I asked about his plans for living together with Kelsie. The more I looked back at it, the more I was convinced something was going on with my cousin. Zane whisked the dressing together and shrugged.

"I don't know, sweetheart. He might feel as though he's not a good provider if he can't afford to get her a big house right now. You know how crazy the market is. I wouldn't read too much into it."

"But where's the fun in that? Of course, Logan's a great provider. He's got his own company. Besides, the new Kelsie isn't that way. She might have been in high school, but she's changed."

"Yes, but is Logan convinced of that?"

I frowned before grabbing the knife to slice up the tomatoes. He had a point.

"I'll ask him about it."

"What did you learn from Sophie?"

My frown cleared as I brought him up to speed on everything we'd learned. By the time I finished, his phone timer dinged, and he grabbed the oven mitts.

"I can't wait to help go over everything. How about we eat first and research after?"

"You know me well."

He carefully placed the piping hot lasagna on the stove and shut the door to the oven. Bernie scooted to the side of the kitchen and started cleaning his face, shooting me a meaningful look in between swipes of his paw.

"Don't forget to tell him about Ned."

I nodded and got our plates out of the cupboard. There was a lot more I needed to say, but right now, the lure of home-cooked food was just too strong. It took everything I had not to dive face-first into my plate as Zane piled it high. We got everything over to the table, and Bernie followed, picking a seat between us, the prime spot for cadging treats.

One bite in, and I thought I had somehow landed in Heaven. I nodded as I chewed, pointing toward my plate with my fork.

"I know I should've started with the salad, but I couldn't resist. Where has this been my whole life?"

Zane blushed, a rare occurrence, before taking another bite. We made quick work of the meal, and yes, I caved. I gave Bernie a small piece of noodle coated with the white sauce and watched as he devoured it whole.

"Did you even taste it?"

"Yes, and it was incredible. More, please."

I translated for Zane while handing over another small piece to my insatiable cat. I groaned as I stood and headed to the kitchen.

"I've got dishes. You don't need to do a thing after cooking up a feast like that."

Zane helped anyway, which he always did. I gave the counters a quick wipe-down and thought about everything I needed to do. Right now, all I wanted to do was take a nap and digest, but that wouldn't help solve our mystery. I forced my feet to walk to the table and pulled out my tote with the printouts.

"Here's everything Sophie found from the paper on the robbery."

"Wow. This seems like a lot," Zane said, eyeing the stack.

"It was big news back in the day, especially since the mine never got its money back. I'm surprised they didn't tear the hills apart looking for it. I think it was tens of thousands that went missing, and that was back then."

"Can you imagine what that would be worth in today's money?"

"I can't. Bernie thinks we should talk to Ned."

Zane nodded slowly as he split the pile of paper in half.

"I know he's not your favorite ghost, but that's not a bad idea. You should see if Mallory wants to go with you. I'd feel safer knowing you had backup. There's no telling what that trickster will pull."

I nodded as I took a seat and pulled my pile closer. We sat in companionable silence for several minutes as we read. I put the pages discussing Jim to one side, figuring they were the most important. Bernie looked over the process, reading over my shoulder.

"There. Right there. That one talks about the lynching."

I swallowed hard as I began reading, the lasagna sitting heavily in my stomach. Mob justice wasn't something I enjoyed reading about, but maybe this would hold a clue. Zane looked up as I gasped.

"What?"

"It says he was hung in the square, but it didn't go according to plan. Something happened when they dropped him. Witnesses described hearing laughter and seeing a strange mist. They had to re-hang Lame Jim."

"That sounds terrible."

"Can you imagine? I mean, I know he robbed the stage and people died, but to be hung twice," I said, shuddering. "But the laughter. The mist. That's kind of what I saw on the ice. There has to be a connection."

Bernie sat straight, his gaze far off, and leapt off the table, jogging toward the back of the house. Zane and I watched him go before looking at each other.

"What was that?"

"I don't know. Whenever he runs back there, he disappears. I'm convinced he's got a portal or something."

Zane didn't blink, which made me smile. No matter how crazy my life got, and it got insane, he rolled with the punches. If I mentioned a portal-traveling cat to anyone else, I'd probably earn a one-way ticket to the funny farm.

"Have I ever told you how much I love you?"

Zane grinned at my conversational shift and stood, tucking his hair behind his ear.

"Yes, but I always love hearing it."

"Let's put this aside and get the rest of your boxes unpacked. I can't believe it's the last."

"I know. I didn't think I had that much stuff, but a lot of this is for work."

"We can put some of this stuff in the back. I've got that closet that should hold it. You can use my storage unit, too, if you need to."

If it wasn't already crammed full of wallpaper, furniture, and antiques, it would be. I winced, remembering it was due for a cleaning. One of the side effects of being a home stager and an interior designer was that I collected stuff. Cool stuff, but it took up a lot of room.

"I think we'll be able to fit it all here. I can put some of it at the office, but it's nice having the higher-value stuff in easy reach."

"Speaking of your equipment," I said, slapping Zane on the arm when he quirked an eyebrow. "Not that. Your camera. I wonder if we could take it to the ice rink and see what it picks up."

Zane had purchased a thermal imaging camera that had captured some pretty spectacular footage when I'd encountered ghosts. His face lit up, and he nodded, excited.

"Great idea!"

We finished getting the boxes unpacked while I kept glancing down the hall, hoping to see my cat. He didn't show, even by the time we were ready for bed. I left the door of my room. Well, I guess it was our room now, open just in case he appeared later. I snuggled into Zane's side and tried to quiet my busy mind. The feeling of Zane's chest rising and falling as he sank into sleep made it easier for me to follow him. My last conscious thought was of Bernie as I slipped under.

7

Some time in the night, Bernie must have returned, given that he was now curled next to my knee, breathing deeply. His tiny kitten snores warmed my heart as I carefully levered up in bed to stroke his head. He cracked an emerald eye in my direction before closing it and snuggling in closer.

"Sorry, bud," I said, whispering as I carefully eased him off my leg. "I have to get up."

"It's an imp."

I paused, one leg still on the bed, as my still-sleepy mind tried to process what Bernie just said.

"A what now?"

"Imp. Look it up. I'm exhausted."

Zane stirred in bed and grinned as he spotted me, half out of bed, hair most likely rioting on the top of my head.

"Is that a new yoga pose you're trying out?"

"Har har. No, Bernie just said something interesting. He said we're dealing with an imp."

"What's an imp?"

Zane was suddenly alert, his eyes sharp as they searched my face. He sat up, revealing his sculpted abs. For a man who liked food as much as he did, it was a miracle he never gained an ounce of fat. What was I talking about? Oh. Yeah. The imp.

"I'm not sure. I guess I'll go look it up. Unless, of course, Bernie would like some breakfast?"

I raised my voice slightly, but Bernie didn't even move. There wasn't much that would keep my cat from eating a hearty meal. I guess he got it from me. I stroked his head again and slid the rest of the way out of bed, clunking my foot down on the wooden floor.

"I'll make the coffee while you do that," Zane said, springing out of bed.

As usual, his long hair looked perfect. I patted the nest on top of my head as I padded down the hall after him, yawning widely. I wasn't a morning person and highly doubted I would ever be afflicted with that problem.

After plopping down at the kitchen table, I reached across and grabbed my laptop, opening it and yawning again. The sound of pots and pans moving around in the kitchen raised my hopes for a home-cooked breakfast. Yep, I could get used to having Zane around.

I focused on the screen and typed in the word Bernie gave me into my browser, frowning as the results came in.

"It says here it's a minor demon, typically associated with mischievous acts. Well, that doesn't sound scary."

Zane chuckled from the kitchen, and I turned my head.

"Only you would put 'not scary' and 'demon' in the same sentence."

"True. I suppose we shouldn't overlook the whole demon part. But still, I was expecting something fearsome, particularly given the laugh I heard."

Sizzling sounds filled the kitchen, and the delicious aroma of bacon hit my nose.

"Remember the ghoul?"

I turned around and saw Bernie sitting in the hall, fur rumpled.

"I thought you were sleeping in. Of course, I remember the ghoul. How could I forget that? But what does that have to do with an imp?"

Bernie heaved a long-suffering sigh and turned his paws toward the kitchen, ending up in front of Zane, where he let out a startlingly loud yowl.

"Dang, buddy. Even I can understand that," Zane said, leaning down to pet the cat. "Chicken? It goes pretty well with bacon."

Bernie chirped and rubbed his head against Zane's leg before shooting me a triumphant smirk. Yeah, we both knew the whole withholding treats thing would not work. Honestly, I was surprised I'd made it nearly twenty-four hours before caving.

"I think that's a yes," I said, snorting, before turning back to my computer. "What do you mean about the ghoul, Bern?"

He stopped winding his way around Zane's legs as Zane dished up his food and looked over at me.

"Keep up, Brynn. The ghoul was once a person who was twisted into that foul being. I think we're dealing with something similar here."

"So, you're saying Lame Jim became an imp?"

Bernie was already nose-deep in his food bowl, so I'd have to wait for my answer. I joined them in the kitchen and watched as Zane scrambled eggs and flipped the bacon.

"Is there anything I can do to help?"

"Want some toast?"

"Sure."

I dropped a few slices of bread into the toaster and grabbed the butter from the fridge while my mind careened around the possibilities. Could a person be turned into a demon? Even a minor demon, like an imp? Did minor demons have the same abilities as major demons? Ugh, I had way too many questions.

"I think I can see smoke coming out of your ears," Zane said, leaning over to kiss me on the cheek. "Let's get some food in you, and then we'll figure it out."

Priorities. I liked the way he thought. I buttered the toast as soon as it popped out of the toaster and stacked it on the plates Zane had on the counter. He scooped some eggs onto my plate, followed by a few strips of bacon. I leaned closer, peering at the eggs.

"What's the green stuff in there?"

"Chives."

"Oh, whew. I thought the eggs went bad."

We grabbed our plates and walked over to the table, visions of domestic bliss dancing in my head. Mundane things, like going to the grocery store, were never fun when I was by myself. But add Zane into the equation, and they suddenly became enjoyable.

Bernie was right on our heels and jumped up to claim his spot, looking at my laptop screen.

"Hmmm. This information is mostly outdated. From what I could learn last night, there's much more to imps than what you can find on the internet."

"Where'd you go?" I asked before forking a pile of eggs into my mouth. "Mmm. These are delicious."

The bright flavor of the chives went perfectly with the eggs. Seriously, I wasn't sure how I'd survived before Zane had come into my life. He'd opened my eyes to so many new things. I guess we'd both done that, since he'd never dealt with the paranormal much in his life before running into me.

"Thanks. I'm glad you like them. What was Bernie saying?"

"Sorry, I got distracted. He said that a lot of the information about imps isn't up to date. I wonder where I could go to get better intel. Bernie? Where did you go last night to learn about it? Maybe you could take me there?"

Bernie's eyes narrowed, and he purposefully looked away, focusing on Zane, watching intently as Zane munched on a piece of bacon.

"No. It's not possible. I think we need to visit Mallory today and take her to Ned. Between the four of us, I think we can find the answers we need."

"Well, I guess I know what I'm doing today. Zane, what do you have going on?"

"I have to run to Creekside and talk to that new client I mentioned. He's still picking out the system he wants, and he needs help deciding. I can put it off if you want me to come with you."

"No. It's fine. Your work is important too. Heck, we may not even be able to find Ned. You know how he is."

We finished our breakfast, and yes, Bernie got his little piece of bacon. From both of us. What can I say? We're both saps. By the time we had the breakfast dishes done and were ready to face the day, the sun was streaming into the living room, where Bernie lay in the center, soaking up its rays.

"I'm assuming you want to go with me?"

He rolled onto his side and tilted his head.

"You would assume correctly. Are you finally ready to go?"

"Yes, Sir Cranky. Hey, you should be in a better mood. You had bacon."

"I'll be in a better mood once we know for sure what we're dealing with. Come on, we're wasting precious time."

I sobered and hurried to the door, grabbing his bag. He was right. The sooner we figured out what was going on at the ice rink, the faster we could ensure no one else got hurt. Zane's hair was still damp from his shower as he joined us. His powerful arms wrapped around my waist, and I breathed in deeply, enjoying the moment.

"Have a good day, and be safe, okay? If you need me, I'll be here faster than you can blink."

"I'll take care of her," Bernie said. "But we appreciate the offer."

I didn't translate his words since my lips were busy with Zane's goodbye kiss. Yep, this whole living together thing was totally worth it. My steps were light as I followed Zane out the door and got in my car. His Jeep pulled away as I got Bernie settled in the passenger seat.

"Well, let's hope Mallory's shop is open. It's pretty early."

"She's there."

I cocked an eyebrow, but Bernie pasted on an innocent face and looked out the window. I was quiet as I drove down the mountain to Deadwood. It wasn't a long drive, but I got stuck behind a snowplow and didn't want to risk passing it. Bernie shifted in his seat and gave me an impatient look.

"Hey, don't look at me like that. Don't crowd the plow. It's like a law or something. We'll be there in two minutes."

All I got for an answer was a disgruntled huff, but luckily, the snowplow turned off, and I could pick up speed right before we reached Mallory's shop. The place looked deserted, and the sign said "closed." I raised my eyebrow at Bernie again, but he shook his head.

"Trust me."

"I always do."

I got out, and Bernie jumped after me, trotting up to the door, where he sat, waiting for me.

I peered inside the window and, sure enough, spotted Mallory moving around within. She turned and made eye contact, smiling widely.

"Brynn," she said as she opened the door. "I was hoping you were coming. Something is really wrong in this town."

"Why? Did something else happen last night?"

She shook her lilac head and frowned.

"I'm uncertain. I wish we had a local paper with a website. All I know is I felt something terrible in the pit of my stomach last night. I can't explain it. I've been listening to the radio, but nothing of import is on there. Just the usual D.J. chatter."

"Oh no. I hope another child wasn't hurt."

Her eyebrows flew up, and I held up a hand.

"Sorry, I should explain. There's something that's been going on at the ice rink. Have you been over there yet?"

She shook her head and leaned against the counter.

"No. I'm not much for skating. What happened?"

Bernie hopped up onto the counter, and she stroked his back while I quickly filled her in on everything we'd learned. Her face clouded as she looked from me over to Bernie.

"An imp? Are you sure?"

"I'm certain."

She let out a ragged breath, and I cocked my head to the side.

"Isn't it just a minor demon? I mean, I know Lame Jim was an evil man, but an imp just doesn't sound that terrifying or powerful."

"You haven't dealt with many demons, and that's a good thing. All I will say is even the smallest demon has more power than any human can imagine. We must act fast. We can't allow it to get stronger."

I looked over at Bernie, who nodded, his face solemn.

"Stronger? What strengthens it?"

"Fear and suffering."

Everything clicked into place. The imp was causing accidents, which could produce both things to get more powerful. A pit opened up in my stomach, and the eggs and bacon sitting there did not appreciate the sensation.

"And you think Ned can help us?"

Bernie nodded as Mallory looked between us.

"Ned?"

"He's the ghost of an old miner who's still around. He hangs out on a mountain, on some land that used to be his. I'll tell you more on the way. Are you up for an adventure?"

She darted behind the counter and grabbed a bright blue puffer coat.

"Always. Let's go meet this ghost."

"I'm going to warn you, he might not be what you expect. I'll drive."

Mallory locked up the store behind us, twirling the keys around her finger like a gunfighter of old.

"The unexpected is always appreciated. I can't wait."

We bundled into the car, and Bernie hopped into Mallory's lap, circling twice before getting settled. I tried to tamp down the sick feeling in my stomach as I left the parking lot. Driving up the mountain to the cabin where Ned liked to hang out wasn't much fun in the summer. I wasn't in a hurry to experience the road in winter, but I had little choice. If this was how we could stop the imp, I would do whatever it took.

8

Even though I'd spent my whole life in these hills, I'm not afraid to say driving in the snow, up a steep mountain, was not one of my favorite things to do. I turned down the car radio and focused on the winding trail, gripping the steering wheel so hard my hands hurt. Mallory leaned up, peering over my shoulder to the cliff's edge, and blanched.

"That's steep."

"You're telling me. It's a good thing I put my all-terrain tires on at the start of winter. You wouldn't want to try this road on worn tires."

"You don't have to worry about that. It is pretty, though."

"Have you gone skiing yet? The resort that's coming up on my left is pretty nice."

Mallory shook her head and bit her lip.

"Can I be honest? I've never skied. I'm worried about looking like an idiot."

I flashed a smile in her direction before focusing back on the road as it switched over to gravel. There were a few more twists and turns, but the elevation leveled out now that we were at the top.

"Don't worry about that. We all have to start somewhere. Tell you what, the next warmish day, I'll bring you up here and we can go down the bunny hills together. It's more fun when you're with a friend."

She nodded, cheeks pink.

"I'm so glad we met and became friends, Brynn. It's tough when you're different. I guess you know all about that, though."

"Yes, us oddballs have to stick together," I said with a wink. "Okay, the cabin is going to be coming up. I don't know if Ned will show up, but he has been around every time I've sought him out. Bernie, do you think you can call him?"

I cruised to a stop and glanced in the back seat where Bernie was looking out the window. He gave a kitty shrug and blinked at me.

"I'll do my best. It looks like we lucked out and the cabin isn't being rented."

Honestly, I hadn't even thought about it, but he was right. Typically, it was a busy rental cabin, but we'd lucked out that it was vacant mid-week. It would have been tough to explain what we were up to if there had been people around. I turned off the engine and rubbed my hands together.

"Ready for this? Like I said, Ned can be a little inappropriate. He looks like a bear, but don't let that throw you. It's just a rug he insists on wearing."

Mallory's eyebrow quirked, and I waved my hand.

"You have to see it to believe it. Bernie, the snow is pretty deep. Do you want me to carry you?"

He chirped his reply, and once I was out of the vehicle, he hopped into my arms, climbing onto my shoulders. I winced as I felt his nails through my down jacket. It was likely going to be full of holes by the time this trip was done.

Mallory walked around, and we stood for a moment underneath a massive pine. The air had that peculiar hush that always seemed to precede a snowstorm. I rubbed my hands together again and nodded.

"We'd better get going. I think we might get a snow squall. I don't want to get caught up here if that happens. It can be perfectly fine down in Deadwood and a blizzard up here."

She nodded and walked toward the cabin, eyes wide.

"So many things have happened here," she said, putting her hand over her heart. "It's almost overwhelming."

I thought back to the poor man who'd been killed at this cabin not that long ago. Luckily, we'd found his killer, and he'd moved on, but it was still a gruesome memory. I shook off the feeling and steered Mallory toward the woods behind the cabin. The shushing sound of our boots through the snow was the only thing I could hear as we entered the tree line.

Bernie gripped me harder, and I felt a gust of wind hit my face. I looked up as the surrounding snow swirled.

"Brynn?"

"It's okay. Ned's here. He's got some... special abilities, you could say. He can manipulate his environment."

Looking at the snow eddy he'd created, that was certainly an understatement. He must have been practicing. I heard a familiar cackle and turned as something loud crashed through the underbrush. Bernie jumped down my back and sat at my feet, fur fluffed up against the cold.

"Girlie, what are you doing out here? Hi, beastie. You're looking fit as ever. It's been a while since you visited old Ned."

I turned to see his familiar stooped form. His craggy face was split with a grin that exposed a mouth of teeth that had never had the benefit of a toothbrush. Ned fascinated me. He was such a contradiction to everything I knew about the spirit world. I think he liked that. I turned to see Mallory, her eyes wide as she stared at the ghost of the old miner.

"And who's this purty gal? What's on her head?"

Ned swooped closer, whipping up the snow in a frenzy as he circled Mallory. She stood her ground and took a deep breath. Her face showed no sign of irritation at being pelted with snow.

"Hello, Mr. Edwards. I'm Mallory Moon. I'm a friend of Brynn's. I dye my hair different colors."

His eyes goggled in his dirty face, and the look he shot me was almost comical.

"She can hear me, too? Well, now this is a rare treat. You a sporting lady?"

"Ned!"

My face must have been crimson based on how hot my cheeks felt. He giggled while he did a little jig. Mallory smiled and shook her head.

"No, I'm not. I'm a psychic."

"Ooo, now that's something you don't see every day," Ned said, peering at her more closely. "Real or fake?"

"She's the real deal," I said, jumping into the conversation. "Ned, do you have time to answer a few questions for us?"

He screwed up his face and drifted closer. Once again, I thanked my lucky stars that smell-o-vision was not an ability I possessed.

"What questions? I'm a busy man."

I resisted the urge to roll my eyes. Ned's version of busy included pestering anyone who rented the cabin or had the misfortune to go exploring in the woods.

"There's no one at the cabin, so I bet you're bored stiff and won't mind helping."

"You do, huh? Well, I'll take that bet. Keep in mind, if I don't think it's worth my time, I might act up a little."

I did not want to see what Ned's version of acting up would be. I held up a hand.

"Did you know a man called Lame Jim?"

Ned spit near my feet, and I reflexively jumped back, even though my logical mind knew he couldn't actually spit. Or maybe he could. There was no telling with Ned.

"I take it that's a yes?" Mallory asked, inching closer. "Why didn't you like him?"

Ned's face took on a mulish expression as he folded his arms. His crooked back made it appear he was folded, staring at the ground.

"He was a wicked man. Haven't heard that name in over a century. Why are you asking about that no-account?"

"We think he might still be around, so to speak," I said, shoving my hands into my pockets to keep them warm.

THE IMP AT THE ICE RINK

Ned straightened as much as he could, and his eyes flared, startling me. I stepped back as Bernie's fur stood on end.

"Where?"

"At the new ice rink in town. There's been, well, there've been a few problems there."

"Ice rink? What's that?"

I took a moment to fill Ned in on the newest attraction in Deadwood and what I'd experienced. By the time I was done, he was shaking his head.

"Don't that beat all? And people pay to glide around in circles in the cold? I swear."

"They do. We tried it. It was fun, minus, of course, the boy who got hurt. Bernie thinks Jim might have turned into an imp."

Ned's eyes immediately went down to where Bernie was still sitting at my feet. Bernie faced off with the temperamental spirit, not backing down.

"Why do you say that, beastie?"

"I've done my research. Do you know what an imp is?"

"Minor demon. Yeah. I've dealt with my share through the years. Girlie, you're in over your head. I recommend you back away and forget about the whole thing. I know I want nothing to do with it. I couldn't stand the man when he was alive, and I reckon I'll like him less now."

The snow swirled again, and I stepped forward, reaching toward Ned.

"Please. Don't leave. We can't let anyone else be hurt. Is there anything you can tell us about Jim that might help us stop him?"

The snow fell all at once as Ned heaved a sigh. His crooked shoulders slumped, and he shook his head.

"Why can't I ever tell you to pound sand? Every time you show up and ask for help, I fold. I know dang well I shouldn't be involved with this."

"Please, Ned. You don't know me, but I sense somehow you'll help to solve this," Mallory said, her face pale. "You're a good man, Ned."

He rolled his eyes and spat again.

"Don't say that too loud, purple hair. I've got a reputation to uphold in these parts."

Bernie circled Ned before stopping and peering at him.

"We'll protect you. I promise. I know you're not ready to head home, not yet. But you still have a responsibility you need to fulfill."

Ned grumbled for a second before his shoulders shook. For a split second, I thought he was crying, but he burst into laughter, startling me yet again.

"Well, when you put it like that, beastie, how can I say no? A cat who's more than a cat made me a promise? Sign me up. Now, tell me the entire story again. Leave nothing out."

Even though the temperature was plummeting and the skies were ominously gray, I obeyed. I included everything we'd learned so far, and Ned listened, nodding. Mallory broke in a few times when I got to the part about imps. Finally, Ned straightened as much as he could and gave a single nod.

"Okay. I'll do it. I'll need some time to gather my energy. You're asking for a showdown, girlie, and that's what you're going to get. I know I can get to Deadwood. I've been there before. I'm not tied here, but it takes a long time to gather the energy to go that far. Give me two days, and I'll do what I can to help. I'm not sure why you need me, but this one here," he said, thumbing in Mallory's direction, "seems to think it's important, and I agree. Meet me at three in the morning on Friday at the Ten. Be prepared. This fight won't be easy."

"Wait, aren't we jumping ahead?" I asked, confused.

"Girlie, you've got a minor demon running loose in Deadwood. Every second we waste is a second he's getting stronger. Do you know how many unsavory characters are still running around that town? What if he recruits them to his cause? He needs to be banished as fast as we can manage it. Do you want to deal with a major demon?"

He vaporized before I could answer. I was so used to his fanfare that it took me a second to realize he was gone. Bernie pawed at my leg, and I picked him up, cuddling him close. Mallory stood, watching the place where Ned had disappeared.

"You were right. He is interesting. Did he mean he'd meet you at ten or three? I don't understand."

"No, he meant Saloon 10 in two days. That's the place where Wild Bill was killed. Well, it's not in the same location it used to be. I wonder if he knows that. I guess the actual spot isn't that far away from the new saloon. We'll find him."

I motioned for Mallory to follow as I headed back through the trees. Tiny flakes of snow hit my face, and I walked faster. We had little time to get back down the mountain before the conditions got worse.

"Do you think we'll actually have a showdown? Like the old days?" Mallory asked, puffing a little as she tried to keep up with me. "And what did he mean about the imp recruiting help?"

"I'm not sure. I have no clue how we're going to pull all of this off. I still don't know for sure what we're dealing with."

She caught up to me and put a hand on my arm.

"I do. I'm here to help. I've got two days to round up a few things that might help. This imp needs to be banished, and we need to make sure it's for good. Who knows what could happen if it continues to gather strength?"

I nodded and gripped Bernie tighter. I was lucky to have so many talented friends. I had a feeling I was going to need all of their skills before everything was said and done.

9

Once we were down the mountain, I breathed a sigh of relief and unclenched my hands, flexing my fingers to get the blood back into them.

"I don't want to do that again," Mallory said. "And I wasn't even driving."

"Me too. I'm really glad Ned said he'd meet us in town. I just wish it wasn't so early in the morning."

"Well, we won't have to deal with anyone at the rink, so that's a bonus. That's a powerful time of day."

"Really?"

Bernie stepped onto the console between us. I glanced down, surprised to see he looked so serious.

"It's the witching hour," he said, his tone solemn. "It's when many things are at their most active. Haven't you ever awakened in a cold sweat and looked at the clock to see it was three? There's always a reason."

A chill raced down my spine, and I huddled into my down jacket.

"He's right. On one side, the imp will be more powerful, but so will our team. We hope."

Mallory's vote of confidence felt a little flat, but I couldn't and wouldn't let it get me down. I had to believe we could do this. I opened my mouth to ask a question, but a call came through my dash, interrupting me.

"Zane? What's up?"

"I'm glad I caught you. You'll never believe what happened."

"I was about to say the same thing. We just met with Ned. I've got Mallory with me."

"Hi, Zane."

"Is everything okay? Hi, Mallory."

"I think so. Ned was well-behaved. He only asked if Mallory was a sporting lady once, so I call that a win. I've got some information, but it sounds like you do, too."

"It's not good news, I'm afraid. You know my new client? The one with the daredevil kid?"

"I do."

"They went skating last night."

My stomach felt like it hit the ground floor of a very tall building in three seconds flat.

"Oh, no. Is he okay?"

"He will be. He broke his leg. My client wants to hold off on the security system for now. It looks like he's going to need surgery, and they weren't expecting something like this."

I covered my mouth as tears sprang into my eyes. We had to do something about this.

"I'm so sorry, Zane. I hope he gets better fast."

"He's young, and they think he'll bounce back. What did you learn?"

"Too much to say over a call. Ned's going to help us. We've got two days to get ready to send this imp back to where it belongs."

"I'll do everything I can. I'm headed up to Deadwood. Meet you at Jill's in an hour?"

"Sure. We can regroup there."

"Later, Sullivan."

"Later, Matthews."

I ended the call and glanced at Mallory. Her face was drawn.

"Another child injured? We can't let this keep happening. What time does the rink open?"

"I think mid-afternoon. Why?"

"We need to go there. Now. Maybe I can pick up on something that will help us."

I studied her face for a second before looking back at the road. I needed to go back to Deadwood to drop her off anyway, so it made sense to stop at the rink first.

"Let's do it. We're only about five minutes away."

She nodded and looked out the window.

"You and Zane are something else. I love the way you can tell him everything, and he doesn't bat an eye. I need someone like that in my life."

"I know. I can't believe how lucky I am."

"Luck has nothing to do with it," Bernie said, stepping into Mallory's lap and turning twice before sitting down. "You found Zane for a reason. Your person is coming, Mallory."

Her eyes went wide, and she looked down at my cat. But he'd closed his eyes and seemed to be sound asleep. Only a cat could drop a verbal bomb and curl up like that. She glanced at me, and I shrugged.

"If he says it will happen, it will. His sense of timing is a little off, though."

I smirked as I caught a sliver of green from Bernie's face as he cracked an eye. I knew he wasn't really asleep. I sobered as I turned near the square and searched for a place to park. From the looks of the lot, we weren't the only ones wanting to check out the rink.

"Bernie, you'd better stay behind. There are far too many people around, and I don't want you getting stepped on."

He abandoned the pretense of sleeping and sat straight up, eyes flashing.

"No, that's not how this is going to work. You've got a tote bag back there. As much as I hate the idea, I'll get inside it, and you can carry me. Gently."

I pulled into the last free spot in the lot. I knew there was no point in arguing with him. I'd lose, badly.

"Okay, but you asked for this. I'll be as gentle as I can."

I dug around in the back until I found the tote bag I stuffed behind my seat. I opened it for him, and Bernie sighed before gingerly climbing in. Mallory watched us, her eyes lit with laughter as he grumbled about his accommodations.

"Bernie, you're a character."

He didn't answer, which I took as a sign to get moving and get this over with as quickly as possible. I slid out of my seat, carefully propping the bag up from below before sliding the strap onto my shoulder. At least my coat was soft and would provide a little cushion on that side. I'd just have to make sure no one jostled me.

Mallory fell into step next to me as we crossed the street. I hung back from the line to rent skates and looked over the rink. You'd never know a string of injuries had happened here, from the happy families circling around, having the times of their lives. A shriek split the air, causing the hair on my neck to stand on end, but I relaxed after seeing the kid go sliding past, yelling for his mom to watch.

"Whew. I thought…"

"I know," Mallory said, her hand on her chest. "I need to go on the ice, but I've never skated. Please tell me you're an old pro at this."

"Um. Well. Not exactly."

She snorted and shook her head.

"So we'll be the blind leading the blind. Got it."

"Zane had some great tips. Maybe that will help. I'd hate to fall and land on my cat, though."

Bernie squiggled in his bag, letting me know what he thought of the idea, and I patted the side.

"We'll be super careful. I feel a pull to the center of the ice."

Her face went pale again as she stared at the rink. I took a deep breath and steered her toward the line. We got behind a family with two young kids and waited our turn. The girl in front of us turned, and her face lit up as she looked at Mallory.

"Are you a princess?"

THE IMP AT THE ICE RINK

Mallory smiled and knelt so she'd be eye to eye with the little girl.

"No, sweetheart. I'm just a regular person."

"You're so pretty," the girl said, reaching to touch Mallory's long hair.

"I'm sorry," the mom said, turning toward us. "She's been on this princess kick lately."

"No worries," Mallory said, giving the girl a little wave before standing. "I love children."

The mother smiled at us before shepherding the little girl in front of her. She peeked around her mother's leg and waved at us before giggling and turning back. My heart clenched at the thought of anything happening to this family, and I said a quick prayer they'd be protected from the imp.

Mallory seemed to sense my thoughts and nodded as she looked across the ice again. Before long, it was our turn, and we rented our skates. I picked the shortest time option, figuring we wouldn't be long, and led Mallory to the benches nearby. I put Bernie's bag down and unlaced my boots. I turned to help Mallory, and by the time I picked the bag back up, it was suspiciously light. I peeked inside and bit back a colorful word.

"He skedaddled, didn't he?"

"Yes. Yes, he did. That little..."

I glanced around, even though I knew it was hopeless. Bernie had a magical way of disappearing when he wanted to, and it looked as though he'd activated it yet again. I sighed and struggled to my feet, balancing on the blades of my skates.

"He'll be okay, Brynn."

"Well, at least if I fall, I won't crush him."

I scanned the grounds one more time before clomping over to the rink's entrance. A group of kids streamed out just as we entered, and I nearly went head over teakettle as one of them jostled me.

"Sorry, ma'am."

I shared a look with Mallory.

"Well, I feel ancient."

We stepped onto the ice, and everything Zane taught me about skating flew out of my head as I tried to remain upright. I took a deep breath and let it out through my nose.

"Okay. I think we need to look forward. You go in the direction you look. I think."

"Makes sense," she said, whooping as she almost fell. "I looked down."

We linked arms and made our way to the center of the ice, watching as children flew around us. Yep, I felt really old. I came to a stuttering stop as a strange sensation danced over my skin. Suddenly, it felt like I'd somehow rolled in nettles. I looked down and noticed the same swirling on the rink's surface.

"Mallory! Do you see that?"

"Yes. I feel it, too. This is bad, Brynn. Real bad."

I risked another look down, and it felt as though I was being pulled forward into a vortex. My stomach heaved as I struggled to remain upright. Everything around me faded into the background, hushing as though someone had covered my ears. I could still hear the surrounding laughter, but it was like I was far away. My vision darkened, and I felt my eyes closing.

"Brynn!"

Bernie's voice shook me out of my trance, and everything came flooding back. I could feel Mallory gripping my arm. Her lips were moving, but I had a hard time focusing on what she was saying.

"We need to get off this ice!"

I nodded as I finally made sense of her words and started retracing our steps. This time, she supported me as we headed for the gate. I looked around but couldn't find my cat.

"Did you hear Bernie?"

"I did," she said, stepping onto the concrete and breathing deeply. "I've got to get out of here."

Panic clawed briefly at my throat, but I ruthlessly pushed back. Now was not the time to fall apart.

"You've got this, Brynn. Focus."

We went back to the bench and found our shoes tucked where

we'd left them, next to the tote bag. My heart skipped a few beats as I got my skates off and rammed my feet into my boots.

Mallory's hands were shaking as she tried to get her shoes on, and I bent down to help. From my spot on the ground, I spotted the tote bag moving.

"Bernie?"

He popped his head out of the bag, and relief washed over me.

"Thank goodness you're back."

"We need to talk."

I nodded as I finished helping Mallory and took our skates back to the check-in desk. She met me on my way back, holding the bag carefully. We were quiet as we headed to the car, lost in our own thoughts. Bernie was right. A demon, even a minor one, was nothing to play with.

10

Bernie was silent until we'd dropped Mallory off. I'd invited her to lunch, but she'd declined, saying she had things she needed to take care of. Nervous energy zipped around my spine, and if it had been possible, I would've parked my car and run all the way home to get rid of the feeling coursing through my bones. It still felt like I'd rolled in nettles. Instead, I did the sensible thing and pulled into the local park. My hands were shaking as I tried to regulate my breathing.

"Do you know how close I came to losing you?"

I turned to look at Bernie, surprised by the sorrow in his voice.

"What do you mean? I just felt a little faint back there. I didn't think it was that serious."

"A little faint, she says," he said with a snarl. "Demons aren't a joke. This isn't just your average ghost we're dealing with. You need to work on shielding yourself."

My lips quirked as I imagined myself lugging around a giant metal shield. That would definitely not be easy to explain.

"Not that kind of shield. I should've known your mind would immediately jump to that."

I spread my hands open and shrugged.

"You know me too well. You can stop peeking in my head, though. That's just weird."

"If you'd learn to shield, it would be a lot harder for me to do that."

I perked up. While I didn't mind my cat sifting through my thoughts occasionally, there were definitely things rattling around in there that I'd prefer he didn't see or hear. I shifted in my seat and checked my watch. I still had another ten minutes before I needed to meet Zane.

"Okay, I'll bite. How do I shield?"

"Imagine your mind is being protected by a large brick wall. I'll give you a second and then try to stop me from entering."

Bernie straightened in his seat next to me and stared into my eyes. I tried to imagine a wall and looked back at him so hard it felt like my eyes were crossing, and he let out a long-suffering sigh.

"It's not working. I can still get right through. We need to work on this."

My stomach grumbled, and I shrugged again.

"Maybe after I've eaten, I'll be able to focus. There's been a lot going on today. You don't mind hanging out in the car while we eat, do you? I know I shouldn't, but I'll bring you something back as a treat."

"Fine. Leave me. Abandon your sole protector in this cold, cold car and go feast to your heart's content."

I turned the key in the ignition and raised an eyebrow.

"Laying it on a little thick there, bud."

"Yeah, that was overkill, wasn't it? I'll be fine. I guess."

I snorted and cruised back onto the street. Jill's Café was our favorite hangout, and with any luck, the sheriff, Dave Beldon, would be around. I wanted to pick his brain and see what he thought about the new ice rink.

Zane's Jeep was already parked in front of the café and I grabbed a spot a few places down, facing toward the sun.

"There you go. I don't want to leave the car running, but now that the storm's gone, the sunlight's coming right in. I won't be too long."

Bernie curled into a ball, wrapping his tail over his nose and said nothing. I scratched behind his ears and turned to see Zane smiling through the window.

"Hey, beautiful. Where's Mallory?"

"She's had something come up. Well, we both did," I said as I got out of the car and shut the door. "We went to the rink, and something happened."

Zane immediately started patting my arms up and down.

"Are you okay? Did you fall?"

"No. We felt something. It was bad. I still feel like it's hanging around. My skin just feels weird."

His dark eyebrows twisted together as he frowned.

"Do you want to go home? We can make some sandwiches there and talk about it."

"No, you can't offer lunch at Jill's and take it away like that. It just isn't fair. I'll be fine. I need to decompress, and this is the perfect place to do that."

His expression said he wanted to disagree, but he nodded and threaded his fingers through mine.

"If you say so. I want to hear all about it, though."

"Later. I just need some food and some friendly conversation that doesn't revolve around demons."

"That makes two of us."

My heart twinged as he opened the door to the café for me. Even though he'd been accepting about what I could do, there was a tiny part of me that held her breath, waiting for the other shoe to fall. Would there be a time when Zane would look at my crazy life and say enough? I tried to shake off my worries, but they clung to my heart with tiny claws.

"Brynn! Long time no see!"

Jill, the owner of the café, bustled toward me, full of energy, as always. I wasn't sure exactly how old she was, but she defied Father Time. Her full poodle skirt swished around her legs. I loved this place. It was as though you'd stepped back in time, a time when clogged arteries weren't really a thing yet. I intended to dive into a burger and not worry about it.

"Hi, Jill. It's good to see you. Two for a late lunch?"

"Hiya, tall, dark, and handsome," she said, elbowing Zane. "Head on to the back booth. Dave's just finished his lunch, and I have a feeling you two need to talk."

She raised a knowing eyebrow and shooed us toward the back. Dave was sitting by himself, staring out the window, his hands wrapped around a cup of coffee. His cowboy hat was on the table, crown up, as always. I slid into the booth across from him and smiled.

"Penny for your thoughts?"

He blinked and gave a gruff nod as Zane joined me.

"Just the two people I was hoping to see. I'm glad you came in here today. We need to talk."

Dave was well aware of my abilities, and we'd worked together on several cases in the past. I'd finally graduated from being embarrassed about what I could do, and I was no longer shy about speaking what was on my mind.

"The ice rink?"

"I should've known you'd already be on top of it. I had a feeling there was more to the story than what the rink owner's been saying."

"Before you talk the poor girl's ear off, let's get some food in her," Jill said, joining us. "Zane's looking a little peaked, too. Bacon cheeseburgers all around?"

She never needed an ordering pad, and most of the time, she didn't even need to take your order. She brought out what she thought you needed. I nodded. She knew me so well.

She tilted her head to the side and looked at Zane.

"You'll have yours with onion rings."

Zane and I shared a smile as she spun around and headed to the kitchen, where she hollered our order across the counter.

"That actually sounds good. I fully intend to steal a few. Don't lock me up," I said, turning back to Dave.

He snorted and took a sip of his coffee.

"What's the rink owner saying?" Zane asked, grabbing some napkins from the dispenser and passing me one.

"After last night, when the call for the ambulance came in, I stopped him and asked him what was going on. He said he couldn't be responsible for clumsy kids, but he was sweating, and he didn't look right. What's going on?"

Jill appeared with two soft drinks, and I unwrapped my straw before answering. Instead of waiting, I dove right in. I explained everything we'd learned so far, and by the time I was done, our food arrived. Jill slid our plates in front of us and took the seat next to Dave, leaning into his shoulder.

Dave wrapped his arm around her and gave her a kiss on the temple. My heart melted a little as I watched them interact. They were the best couple. What? Who set them up? Yours truly, and I was still giddy over it.

Zane handed over an onion ring and snagged the ketchup from me. I bit into the fried goodness and nodded my head. I'd forgotten how good the rings were here. Jill watched us with a little smile on her face.

"See? I knew you wanted the onion rings. At least you're both going to eat them, if you know what I mean."

She let out a cackle, and I blushed a little before biting into my cheeseburger. I'd added a little too much ketchup and reached for a napkin.

"How dangerous is this spirit? You think it's got something to do with an old robbery?"

I nodded while I dredged a fry through the lake of ketchup on my plate.

"I do. I still need to do more research, but I believe it's connected to the hanging of Lame Jim. Is it true he had to be hung twice?"

Dave ran a hand over his balding head.

"It's been a long time since I heard that story, but I think you're right. I wonder what happened?"

"I don't know, but we need to find out. I have a theory, but I'm still kicking it around."

We finished our meals in silence while Jill and Dave talked about the different robberies that happened back in the day. A few stories were fresh to me, and some were fairly recent.

"I can't believe how much history is in this town," Zane said, wiping his mouth. "Thank you for the amazing food, Jill. Excellent as always."

She gave a quick nod before hopping up to clear away our plates. I finished the last of my drink and stared down at my hands as a thought occurred to me.

"You said the owner of the rink was acting weird. What did you mean?"

Dave picked up his hat and worked his hands around the brim, his brow furrowed.

"I don't know. I've known Ted for a few years, but he's never been like this. He was all sweaty and kept looking around like something was haunting him. I think it'd be a good idea if you talked to him."

"Does he have an office near the square?"

"No. It's down in Creekside. I don't know why, so don't ask. He's typically around in the morning. I'd appreciate it if you'd look in on him and see what he says. Maybe it's all in my head."

"I'll do that tomorrow. Let us know if anything else happens."

"I will. I'll have a man monitoring the rink, just in case. Some of these incidents didn't require an ambulance. That poor boy last night sure did, though. I'd heard a few rumors, but that was the first serious accident."

"I hope it's the last," I said, folding my napkin. "We've got two more days until Ned can help. I don't know exactly what's going to happen, but we're going to do our best."

"You know about that stuff more than I do, but if I can help, I'll do it. Three in the morning, you said?"

"Yep. It's going to be a long night."

"Well, I'll be there as backup. Just in case."

Warmth flooded my soul as he nodded and slid out of the booth. Having friends you could count on was something more valuable than gold or the payroll from a mine. I turned to Zane as he took some money out of his wallet and put it on the table.

"Hey, I thought it was my treat?"

"Nope. Not today. What do we do now?"

I thought for a second before an idea popped into my head.

"I know just the thing. How do you feel about doing some demo at the little house? Breaking down a few walls sounds like just the ticket."

"I like the way you think. I'll follow you up there."

I followed him through the café, waving to Jill as we exited onto the sunny street. It was just warm enough that the snow from earlier had melted. I patted the pocket where I'd stowed Bernie's treat and walked with Zane to my car. He held open the door and pulled something out of his pocket, giving me a wink.

"I saved him something, too."

I laughed as I took it and got in. Zane shut the door for me and winked on his way back to his Jeep. I doled out the treats and headed to the little house. Maybe while I was breaking down some walls, I could work on building some in my head. I'd promised Bernie I'd practice. It was worth a try.

11

Do you know that feeling where you are bone-tired, but your brain just won't turn off? That's where I was as I lay in bed, staring at the ceiling, listening to my cat and my boyfriend saw logs. I flipped my pillow over for the third time and let out a slow breath of air, running through the events of the day.

Tearing out the old kitchen at the house in Coppertown with Zane had been fun. What's not to love about taking out frustration on innocent cabinets and walls? We'd scarfed down a quick dinner and spent some quality time with Bernie, watching television and not thinking about the imp. Well, maybe it's better to say we'd tried not to think about the imp. Ned's warning kept whispering in the back of my mind.

I turned on my side and tried holding my breath for a few counts before letting it out. Yeah, this wasn't working. I slowly slid my legs out of bed and tiptoed toward the door.

"Brynn? Are you okay?"

I winced before nodding. Zane couldn't sleep through much, and I should've known I'd wake him.

"I'm fine. Just restless. I'm going to get some water."

Soft snores were my only response. Envy pierced my chest as I walked to the kitchen. If only it were that easy. I poured myself a glass of water and leaned against the kitchen cabinets. I tried practicing building my mental wall, but it wasn't nearly as fun when I didn't have Bernie telling me I was doing it wrong. I drained my glass and looked around the kitchen, spotting the stack of papers Sophie had given me the day before.

Well, since I was up, maybe reading through the events of the robbery would be a good use of time. I grabbed the pile and headed for the living room, flipping on the table lamp. I'd forgotten to call Sophie to ask about her luck in getting a cat from the shelter. I'd have to do that tomorrow.

I began reading and soon was completely engrossed in the story of Lame Jim and his band of troublemakers. Whoever had written the story had a way with words that captivated me, making the over-century-old events feel as though they were happening right outside my door.

I turned to another article and sat straight up as I read and then re-read the passage again.

"What are you doing?"

"Gah! You scared the holy heck out of me, cat. How do you do that?"

"Hey, I chirped to let you know I was here. It's not my fault if you didn't hear me."

Bernie hopped onto the couch and snuggled in his favorite spot on my feet, peering into my lap. I stroked his head as I read through the article again.

"It says here that Lame Jim's sister was known as 'the woman of the woods' and feared by many of the locals as a witch. She was much older and raised him when their parents died. Do you think?"

"We finally found the link we were missing. Keep going."

My heart rate sped up as I dove back into the article. I was silent until I'd finished it. My fingers shook a little.

"So, from all appearances, Lame Jim was deeply involved in the occult."

"I wonder if that's why they never found the money he stole. He might have been powerful enough to create a glamour or a shield to hide it from prying eyes. I have a feeling that loot is tied to all of this. That and the fact they had to hang him twice."

"What do you mean?"

Bernie repositioned himself. Now was not the time to tell him one of my feet had fallen asleep. I'd just have to deal with the pins and needles until he got to the point.

"Okay, so his sister was most likely a witch. He probably had some abilities, too. However, in most witch family lines, the power is much stronger in the females. Males can have power, but it's typically muted. If you ask me, which you did, I think he made a bargain with some dark forces for more power. He might have allowed an imp to possess him to help him reach his goals."

"So witches are real?"

"That's your takeaway from all of that?"

"I don't know. I always thought the word was created by small-minded people who didn't understand the paranormal," I said, holding up my hands. "I need to move, bud. I can't feel my foot."

He stood up slowly, because of course he did, and moved into my lap. I swiveled my legs around and rolled my foot back and forth, wincing as the feeling returned to it in a rush.

"You're right on some counts. A lot of gifted individuals get labeled a witch when they aren't. But yes, witches are real. So are warlocks. So are people who barter their souls, which was the important part of what I said."

"Sorry, I got distracted. So, you think Lame Jim sold his soul for what?"

"Wealth. It's a tale as old as time, Brynn. Greed knows no bounds with some people."

"Okay, that makes sense. But why is it suddenly starting now? Lame Jim died over a century ago."

Bernie tilted his head to the side and shifted, digging his back claws into my lap as he got comfortable.

"My guess is the second hanging had something to do with it. The imp, which is most likely entwined with Lame Jim's soul, was weak after that. It might have lain dormant until something happened. Was anyone injured during the construction of the rink?"

"I don't know, but that's a question I can ask the owner. I plan on visiting his office tomorrow," I said, glancing down at my watch. "Or, I guess today. I didn't know it was this late. I should try to get a little sleep."

I wrapped my arms around him and struggled to get to my feet in a graceful motion. Let's just say it didn't go well.

"Wait, I'm not done. The money. We need to find the money."

I paused, hand on the switch of the lamp, and looked down at my cat.

"What? Why?"

"It's involved. Trust me. We need to find it so we can banish Lame Jim and the imp. For good. Until that connection is removed, they both might come back."

"Oh, okay. We'll just somehow find money that's been hidden for more than a hundred years. Money that the Pinkertons and all the professionals searched for and couldn't find. Easy peasy."

I swear I could feel Bernie rolling his eyes. I put him down on the couch and he spun around, facing me, green eyes bright.

"We have tools they didn't have."

I took a seat next to him, mind racing. I mean, yeah, finding buried treasure was a childhood dream, especially growing up near Deadwood. There were so many legends of gold buried in the hills. My cousin had spent years as a teenager convinced he was going to strike it rich and find some.

"Logan. We could get him to help."

"Well, he can certainly be the brawn. I'm the brains. Good idea. He's good at digging."

I grabbed my phone off the table and fired off a text to my cousin. I was about to put it back down when I saw he was typing a response. I glanced at my watch again, brow furrowed. Why was he up so late? I flipped my phone to silent before his text came through.

"You're kidding, right? Why are you still up?"

"Long story. Tell you tomorrow. Are you in? And why are you up?"

This time, it took a lot longer for Logan to answer. I watched the three dots on our message window for what felt like an eternity before his text came through. It was brief.

"I'm in."

I tapped my fingers on the side of my phone as I reined in my desire to pry into what was going on with my cousin. He hadn't answered the important question. Was everything okay with him? I groaned softly and sent over the thumbs-up emoji and put my phone down. My cousin's issues would keep until morning. I turned back to Bernie.

"He'll help. Where do we look?"

"Leave that to me. I have some resources I can tap."

"Resources? What resources?"

He thumped down from the couch and looked at me over his shoulder.

"Now's not the time. I know we need to talk and we will. I promise. We need to focus on this first. Let's go back to bed and get some rest. I have a feeling we're going to need it. And you need to work on shielding."

It took me a second to realize the last part of his sentence hadn't been spoken physically but in my head. I grimaced as he walked out of the room, tail held high.

"You little..."

I shook my head as I shut the light off and trailed after him. Zane murmured as I got into bed, pulling me close. This time, even though my mind was full of questions, the soft snores from Zane lulled me into a deep sleep almost instantly.

The next thing I knew, I was standing in a dark forest. A flickering light in the distance was like a siren song. I took a few steps toward it before realizing my feet made no sound on the forest floor. What on earth? My skin prickled as I moved again.

The flickering got my attention again, and I drifted toward the light, intrigued. I came to a stop, hidden behind a towering pine, and watched as a man flung dirt out of a hole in the ground. He was stripped to the waist, his thin frame exposed to the icy wind that whipped through the trees. I dared another step closer as he kept digging. He was talking to himself, swearing as he flung more dirt out of the hole. Bulging saddlebags were piled around the edges, their leather cracked and worn.

"There. That should be deep enough," he said, levering himself out of the hole.

He stood for a second, looking down at what he'd dug. His face was drenched in sweat, but I'd have known it anywhere. Whoever made the wanted posters back then was definitely a talented artist. He pushed the bags into the hole and started kicking dirt onto the top of them. I risked one more step forward and paused as a branch under my feet cracked.

Lame Jim's eyes snapped over to me and I froze as I glimpsed the madness within their depths. I was in trouble. Big-time trouble. My feet refused to move as he stood, never taking his eyes off me.

"You! What are you doing here?" he asked, howling the words.

I stammered as he closed the distance between us. I could smell the rank sweat dripping from his face as he grabbed for me. There was something wrong with his eyes. Where his irises should have been was full of flames. My stomach shriveled into a tiny ball and my lungs refused to work.

Why wasn't I waking up? This is the part of the dream where I'm supposed to wake up, right? His hands felt like vise grips as they closed around my shoulders and I screamed, terrified.

12

Everything went black, but the sound of screaming remained, echoing through my ears. On the plus side, I couldn't see Lame Jim's horrible eyes. Unfortunately, I could see nothing.

"Brynn! Stop! You're safe."

I closed my mouth, and the screaming finally quit. It took me a second to put everything together. Zane flipped the light on, and the first thing I registered was the terrified look on his face. Bernie was at the foot of the bed, arched into an almost impossible arc, hair standing on end.

"Sorry. Sorry. I didn't know I was still screaming."

Zane's chest heaved as he climbed back into bed and wrapped his arms around me.

"I thought I was dreaming until I woke up and heard you. I shook you, but you wouldn't stop."

I could feel the tremor in his voice as he held me to his chest. Bernie's whiskers brushed my arm as he crowded close.

"What did you dream? I need to hear everything, from start to finish."

"Hang on a second, Bern. Let my heart rate come back to normal," I said, raising a hand to brush the sweaty hair off my face.

"I don't want you to forget anything."

He placed a paw on my leg, and I peeked under Zane's arm to meet his eyes. There was no way I was going to forget anything that happened, but he had a point. I took a shuddering breath and leaned back. Zane seemed reluctant to release me.

"What does he want?"

"He wants to hear about my dream. Maybe it's important. I think it was just what I read before bed, but who am I to disagree with my cat?"

I scooted back and fluffed up my pillow so I could lean against it. Zane joined me, wrapping an arm around my shoulders and using his other to pull the covers up over us. Bernie waited impatiently at my feet.

"Okay. So I was standing in the forest..."

"Where?"

"Um. I don't know. There were a lot of trees."

"Very helpful."

"I could tell you my dream a lot faster if you didn't interrupt, cat."

"Proceed."

I narrowed my eyes at Bernie while he pasted an innocent expression on his face. It faded as I retold what I saw. His green eyes were bright as I told him about what I saw in Jim's eyes.

"That's it. You were seeing the moment he buried the treasure. I told you I had resources."

I screwed up my face as I translated his words for Zane. My ever-patient boyfriend looked lost.

"I don't understand. What now?"

"Oh. I should probably tell you about what we found out earlier when I couldn't sleep."

By the time I was done laying everything out, Zane was nodding.

"Okay, it's a big jump, but if Bernie says it was real, I believe him. He's never wrong."

Bernie shot me a triumphant look, and I shook my head. Just what he needed: an even bigger ego.

"Are you sure I wasn't just working through everything I learned? The mind is a funny thing."

"You heard the man. I was right. And I always am."

"Yeah, yeah. Okay, let's assume I just saw where Lame Jim buried the treasure. How are we going to find it? I just saw trees. There weren't any defining features of the landscape. All my dream did was confirm he buried it somewhere in the Hills, which we already knew. And it scared the holy heck out of me."

"You're not the only one," Zane said, rubbing my arm. "I never want to hear you scream like that again. I thought my heart was going to stop."

"Let me in. I'll sift through your memories and find the place. We can narrow it down," Bernie said, coming closer.

"What now? Sift? I don't know if I like that word."

"What's he saying?"

"Something about sifting through my brain. Look, cat, maybe that can wait till morning? It's after four as it is."

Bernie came closer and put a paw on my knee.

"Trust me, Brynn. It will be okay. Don't forget, cats have built-in GPS."

I grumbled a little, but who was I kidding? We've already established I'm terrible at saying no to my cat. I took a deep breath and closed my eyes, waiting. After a second of nothing, I cracked open an eye and looked at Bernie.

"Well? Start sifting."

Zane chuckled and held my hand. I squeezed it as I closed my eyes again. Bernie heaved a sigh.

"You're so dramatic."

"*I'm* dramatic?"

"Hush. Focus on your dream again."

I bit my lip and tried to recall every detail I could while Bernie did his thing. Honestly, I really couldn't tell if he was in there sifting around. Whatever that entailed. I didn't need details.

"Got it. We can start our search tomorrow."

I translated for Zane, who stared at Bernie.

"You can do that? See an image and tell where it's at?"

Bernie walked down to the end of the bed and stretched, vibrating the bed a little. He got comfortable and wrapped his tail around his eyes.

"Yep. Within a half mile or so."

"Cat, you're amazing."

"See, he gets me," Bernie said, cracking an eye before closing it and snuggling close to my foot.

"I'll get you," I said, even though we both knew I was kidding.

"What now?" Zane asked.

I leaned forward and grabbed my pillow, fluffing it back into shape. Even though I'd been wired, my eyes were heavy, and sleep was pulling at me.

"Let's go back to bed and try for another few hours, at least. There's not much we can do right now. I want to visit the owner of the rink tomorrow, and then, well, it looks like we're going on a treasure hunt."

"This is so exciting. I feel like a kid again. I have nothing going on tomorrow, so I can help you."

I yawned and struggled to stay awake.

"I texted Logan. He's been wanting to find buried treasure since we were kids. He'll help. We can let him do the digging."

"Sounds like a plan."

He wrapped himself around me, and I floated away on a peaceful cloud. I had a sneaking suspicion Bernie did something to my head to help me sleep, but right now, that was the furthest thing from my mind.

I WAS EXPECTING to wake up on the cranky side of the bed, given how little sleep I'd gotten, but as soon as the sun was up, there I was, bright-eyed and bushy-tailed. Zane groaned as he followed me to the kitchen. His long hair lay perfectly on his head, while mine... well, let's just say I should've put it in a braid before falling asleep and leave it at that.

Luckily, Zane was used to my morning appearance and said nothing, kissing me on the top of my head before going to the cupboard to get Bernie's food ready. I made a beeline for the coffee pot and tossed in an extra scoop for good measure.

"We need a nutritious breakfast if we're going to be looking for treasure," Zane said, scooping Bernie's food into his bowl. "Let me check the fridge."

"You're amazing. If it were up to me, I'd grab a granola bar and head out the door, but you always think ahead."

Zane beamed at me before poking his head in the fridge.

"I love taking care of you. All right, we've got eggs, sausage, and let me check... yep, we've got tortillas. Does a breakfast burrito sound good?"

"It sounds way better than good."

We fell into our usual cooking routine, where Zane did the heavy lifting and I provided support. Hey, I may burn water, but I can whisk eggs pretty well. Before I knew it, he was rolling up our burritos while Bernie sat at his feet, eyes wide.

"I just fed you. You can't possibly be hungry," Zane said, pinching off a piece of egg and handing it over.

"He takes after me," I said, grabbing both plates and heading for the table.

Zane topped off our coffee mugs before following me to the table. We ate in silence, devouring our burritos. Bernie paced restlessly by the front door as we cleaned up our mess.

"It's going to be a few minutes, bud," I said, wiping down the counters. "We still need to get dressed."

"Well, hurry. We need to get into the woods before we run out of light. You know how quickly the sun sets this time of year."

I saluted him and rolled my eyes as I turned around. He had a point. Zane followed me back to our room, and we got dressed, forgoing our usual shower. By the time we were done, Bernie had already loaded himself into his bag by the door.

"Finally. Let's go."

I grabbed his carrier and zipped it up, marveling that he wasn't fighting about being allowed to roam free in Zane's Jeep. I wasn't about to bring it up, though, and quickly hustled out to the car. Zane cranked the heat, and we headed out.

"Do you know what you're going to ask the owner? What was his name?"

"Ted. I need to look up his last name. I want to find out just how many incidents there have been, and I want to see if anything unusual happened during construction. I have a feeling it's connected to Lame Jim's sudden appearance."

I pulled out my phone while Zane turned onto the highway, heading to Creekside. It took me a few minutes, but I could finally piece everything together.

"Okay, his name is Ted London. He's a lifer in the Hills. Before owning the rink, he owned a clothing store that went belly up. I wonder what made him go into this business?"

"We'll have to ask. The office is downtown, right?"

I pointed out the turn, and we found a spot to park. I turned and looked in the backseat where Bernie was sitting quietly. Too quietly.

"You have had little to say. Is everything okay?"

"I'm communing with the spirits."

"Really?"

"No. I was grabbing a nap. It's going to be a long day."

I rolled my eyes again as I got out of the Jeep and grabbed his bag. I knew without asking he wanted to come with us into Ted's office. I could only hope no one was going to ask why I was carrying a bag.

Zane looked around the building's lot, which was almost empty. The only other car was a brown sedan with dirt encrusted around the tires.

"I hope he's around."

"Me too. Maybe I should have made an appointment."

I bit my lip as we went into the entrance. The mailboxes confirmed this was Ted's office, so I headed up the stairs to number four and hoped for the best. A light was on! I pumped my fist and grinned at Zane before rapping on the door.

"Yes? Who is it? What do you want?"

A man popped his head out of the door, and I took a step back. If this was Ted London, he'd definitely seen a better day. His skin was pale and his eyes darted back and forth, looking down the hallway.

"Are you Ted London?"

He nodded before catching himself. Zane smiled and stuck out his hand.

"Zane Matthews with Matthews Security. Do you have a few minutes?"

Those seemed to be magic words to Ted London's ears. He brightened and waved us in. I didn't miss the way he looked down the hall before closing the door firmly, locking us in the tiny space. What was going on?

"I can't believe it! Did George send you? I was going to call you and see if you could help with a new project, and here you are. It's a miracle!"

Ted's voice rose an octave as he ended his sentence. I couldn't bear to be the one to crush his hopes and looked over at Zane. Ted wrung his hands as he looked at Zane like someone who hadn't seen the sun in way too long. Zane swallowed hard and smiled.

"Take a seat, Mr. London, and let's talk. It sounds like you've got something on your mind."

Ted nodded like a bobblehead and raced behind his desk, motioning for us to take the chairs opposite it. I sank down and tucked Bernie's bag by my feet. I couldn't wait to see what Ted had to say.

13

Having just met Ted London, I didn't know if the clutter in his office was new, but it was certainly a window into his current mental state. Piles of papers were everywhere, making the small space feel even smaller. Dust coated his desk, and there was a stale smell hanging in the air. I shifted in my chair as Ted began talking.

"I can't tell you how grateful I am that you're here," he said, wiping his forehead. "I don't know how much longer I can take it."

"Take what?"

"That's the thing," Ted said, banging his fist on the table so loudly I jumped. "I don't know what's going on, but I need help. I'm not afraid to ask for it. I can't handle one more thing happening at the rink. I just don't understand what's going on."

Zane held up a hand and leaned forward.

"Why don't you start at the beginning?"

"Right. Right. Good idea. I'm sorry, I'm all over the place lately. Long story short, I contracted with the city to install an ice rink. I've done nothing like this, but last year, my family took a trip over to Europe to see some long-lost relatives, and while we were over there, I saw this new system for ice rinks. It was revolutionary. I'd just sold my other business and was looking for something new, and it hit me. Why not bring this new technology to America? One of the major problems with ice rinks is the cost of maintenance and dealing with weather changes. I knew Deadwood had wanted to add a rink for years, especially to help with winter tourism, but the costs had been too prohibitive. In warmer years, when the ski industry takes a hit, they still need to bring people in. It was the perfect solution. Did you know it's the first rink of its kind in the state?"

Zane smiled and gave the nervous London an encouraging nod.

"I didn't, but I do now. What kind of business did you have before? Sorry, I'm new in town, and I don't know all the ins and outs of everyone."

"Oh, sure. I had a restaurant here in Creekside. My dad started the business years ago, and we built up a loyal following. In fact, the manager was with us for thirty years and saved up enough to buy me out. I thought I'd have enough experience to run a rink. I mean, it's customer-facing, and we have concessions. I thought it would be a piece of cake. I never imagined it would be like this."

Ted trailed off and pivoted his chair toward the window. The harshness of the sunlight illuminated his wrinkles. He looked like a man in serious need of rest, hydration, and time off. I knew from my brief look at his background on our way here he was in his late forties, but right now, he looked like he was pushing sixty.

"There've been reports of several injuries at the rink. My girlfriend, Brynn, and I were present for one of them," Zane said, nodding toward me.

Ted's eyes flickered over to me for a second before he refocused on Zane. He grimaced and nodded.

"The last one may break me. The city is talking about shutting me down. Even though the liability waiver is in force, I still can't let that boy's parents shoulder the load for his hospital bills. I offered to pay at least half. I've invested everything in the rink. Everything. I don't even own the land, so it's not like I can recoup much if it all goes belly-up. It's gotta be sabotage. That's the only explanation."

I scooted forward in my chair.

"Why do you say that?"

Ted met my eyes, and my heart twisted at his tortured expression.

"It has to be. There's no other earthly explanation. From day one, there's been nothing but problems. It's almost as if I'm cursed. I sank my daughter's college fund into this project."

His shoulders heaved, and he squeezed his hands together. Zane cleared his throat.

"Do you have any enemies who would want to see you fail?"

Ted's eyes briefly brightened before he shook his head.

"That's the thing. I thought I was well-liked. I mean, I've lived here my whole life. I'm more well-known here than in Deadwood, but our towns aren't that far apart. I can't think of anyone I've angered. I've been up too many nights thinking about it."

"When you say from the start, what happened?" I asked.

"Well, the installation process for the rink itself is pretty straightforward," Ted said, running a hand through his hair. "It's not terribly difficult. You install each section and move to the next, like a giant puzzle. But nothing went right after we broke ground in the square. We had to pour the concrete foundation twice. It was the strangest thing. We poured it, and it was all cracked when it cured. It all had to be ripped out and replaced. That set us back a month, which is why the rink opened so late. We were shooting for Christmas. After that, pieces of the material went missing. Tubes went inoperable. One of my men was injured in a freak equipment accident. It just makes little sense. Once it was finally all assembled and ready to go, I thought we were in the clear. But it's been one bad thing after another."

He banged his fist down again. My heart went out to the guy. I wished I could tell him what was really going on, but I wasn't sure hearing the cause was supernatural was going to help him relax. If anything, it would make it worse. My best guess was that when they were digging, they somehow released the imp. Ted continued, leaning over his desk toward Zane.

"I told my friend George Halwell that I feel like I'm losing my mind. He'd heard good things about you and recommended I call you. Maybe there is someone out there who hates me enough to do this. But why would they hurt children? Why? I'll pay you whatever you want if you can fix this for me. I've got a little stashed away for emergencies, and if you can stop it, I'll find more. You've got to believe me."

Zane shook his head.

"Let's not worry about that right now. With your permission, I'd like to set up some surveillance equipment. It might take a few days. I understand it's a busy attraction during the day and evenings, so I'll need access at night."

"Whatever you need, you have my carte blanche. I just don't want anyone else hurt. I've shut the rink down until we figure out what's going on."

Zane stood and held his hand out to Ted, who grabbed it like a lifeline. For the first time since we'd met him, he smiled.

"I'll keep you updated."

Ted saw us out, tears running down his cheek as he shook Zane's hand again. I grabbed Bernie's bag and followed Zane out to the parking lot, holding my tongue. That had been totally unexpected.

Once we were safely in the Jeep, I released Bernie and looked over at Zane.

"Well, I guess that solves our problems of being at the rink at three in the morning. You're a genius."

I kissed Zane on the cheek and bounced a little in my seat.

"I have my moments. There's no way I can charge him, but at least we have access to the site, and no one can question us. The poor guy, I thought he was going to fall apart in there. I didn't have the heart to tell him we weren't there to help him."

"I know. We learned nothing new, but at least we confirmed the problems started when construction began."

"You should've asked him if they found something while they were digging. I'm guessing there was a vessel of some sort that contained the imp," Bernie said from his spot in the backseat.

I spun around and shrugged.

"I know, but he's a man on the edge. I didn't want to be the one to send him over by talking about woo-woo stuff."

THE IMP AT THE ICE RINK

"It's not woo-woo if it's real."

"You know what I mean, Bern. At least we know he's trying to fix the problems and not just a negligent business owner. I mean, we have to look at all sides."

Bernie sniffed and licked at his flank. I turned back to Zane as we pulled out of the lot.

"It's hard to believe. There's even more riding on this than we thought," Zane said.

"I know. Poor Ted and his family. And all the poor kids who've been hurt. We can only hope our team will be strong enough to take this imp out. We've only got one more day to prepare, and I'm still not sure what role I need to play."

Worry clawed at my throat as I thought about it. I knew Mallory was working on getting prepped, and Ned was bolstering his energy, but what was I supposed to do? I couldn't just sit back and hope for the best.

"So let's go find some buried treasure. We're going to use it to trap the imp. I've got it all planned out," my cat said.

Both of us turned to look at Bernie, sitting smugly in the backseat, little chest puffed out. Zane looked back to the road and smiled at me after I translated Bernie's words.

"You gotta love his confidence. Alright, cat. Do your thing. You said you can get us within a half mile?"

"I'd probably get you a lot closer if there was a hamburger involved," Bernie said, passing a paw over an ear as he bathed.

"How much closer are we talking?" I asked, rolling my eyes.

"How many holes do you feel like digging?" Bernie shot back.

"He's got a point. Let's grab an early lunch and we'll follow his lead. Once we're there, I'll call Logan and get him to help."

"Sounds like a plan. Hey, there's that new burger place on the way. Let's stop there and get lunch to go."

"I'll have mine with bacon, please."

I glanced back at Bernie as he shot me a triumphant look. Even though I had no clue where we were headed or how we were going to find a proverbial needle in a haystack, I couldn't tamp down the excitement rising in my chest. An honest-to-goodness treasure hunt? I mean, what are the odds?

I sang along to the radio as Zane headed down the highway. Even though we were about to be facing the fight of a lifetime, I was determined to live in the now and appreciate this moment. Fear and worry could wait, at least for a few hours. We had some treasure to find.

14

After what felt like ages, but was really only about half an hour, we came to a stop in the trees. Even though it was cold, I was sweating underneath my down jacket and wishing I'd brought some different layers. Hey, it's not like I'd actually gone on a treasure hunt before. Next time, if there was a next time, I'd be more prepared.

I heaved a sigh and spun slowly in place, looking at the trees. I had to hand it to Bernie. It looked remarkably like the spot I'd seen in my dream. Unfortunately, a lot had changed in the past hundred years, but something about the place felt right.

"You didn't bring any shovels?"

I winced as I looked down at Bernie. Okay, I was super unprepared.

"No. I didn't think of shovels this morning. In my defense, having a wild dream kind of distracted me. And anyway, I only have one."

Zane looked between us like he was watching a high-stakes tennis game. He raised a hand.

"I'm pretty sure your cousin, who owns a construction company, can bring extra shovels. We won't start until he's here."

I pointed at Zane while nodding at my cat.

"Yeah, Zane's right."

"Amateurs. I'm surrounded by amateurs. If I had thumbs…"

"I know, I know. You'd rule the world. Let me text Logan."

I pulled out my phone, and to my surprise, I had service. I fired off a text with a request for some extra shovels and a map pin for our location before tucking my phone back in my pocket. Bernie was still muttering about my utter lack of preparation, and I tuned him out. He was right, but that didn't mean I wanted to hear it.

I walked toward the clearing and put my hands on my hips. Now that I had cooled down, I was happier than I was wearing my heaviest coat. The wind whipping through the pines chilled my flushed face. Zane sidled next to me and wrapped an arm around my waist.

"How long do you think it will take Logan to get here?"

"Hard to say. Probably half an hour. At least we found the general spot. I'm just trying to piece it all together from what I remember of the dream."

"Take your time," he said, rubbing his hand up and down my back. "It will come. I believe in you."

I shot him a quick smile before focusing back on the clearing. Seeing it in broad daylight, with the mature trees, threw me for a loop. I walked forward, stepping carefully.

"I think this might be the spot to start," I said.

Bernie stalked over, using my footprints to hop as he'd been doing the whole time he directed us to this location before settling at my feet. I picked him up and wrapped an arm around him to block the chill. He leaned his head against my neck briefly before looking around.

"It feels right. There's power here. It's old, but its remnants linger. We'll need to tread carefully in case Lame Jim laid a trap."

"Trap?"

"Trap? What's he saying?" Zane asked.

"He thinks Lame Jim might have laid a trap for anyone who might find the treasure."

"That doesn't include the glamour he cast on the spot," Bernie said, raising his nose to scent the air. "It led me right to the spot. The magic is old, but it's there."

"You can smell magic?"

Bernie didn't answer, and I heaved another sigh. Let him keep his secrets. For now, anyway. Eventually, I'd ferret them out. We walked around in a circle as I tried to orient myself. Bernie struggled out of my arms and leapt to the ground, ignoring the deep snow as he plowed through it.

"Here. Right here. I need to check something."

He closed his eyes, and I stepped in front of Zane. I didn't know what kind of magical trap Bernie was talking about, but I wanted to be the one to absorb it, not Zane.

"What do you think you're doing?" he asked, his tone full of laughter.

"Protecting you. I know you are way taller, but I have to hope the magic would come for me first."

He put his hands on my shoulders and kissed the top of my head before spinning me around.

"I appreciate the gesture, but I can't contemplate life without you."

Any trace of chill I was feeling fled as my heart warmed in my chest. I stood on my tiptoes and kissed Zane on the cheek.

"If you two are done with the PDA, I think we're okay. There was a hint of something left behind, but it's long gone."

I blushed and refocused on my cat. He picked his way through the snow and sat on my boot, curling his tail around his paws.

"Here, I'll take him. I've got room in my coat," Zane said, reaching down for my cat.

He unzipped his coat with one hand and tucked Bernie inside, cradling him with his other arm.

"I need to buy him a coat if we're going to keep going on these winter adventures outdoors. I don't want him to get sick."

Bernie popped his head out of Zane's coat and shot me a look.

"I'm fine. I don't get sick like an ordinary cat."

"Because you're a guardian?"

Bernie's eyes narrowed, and he muttered while burrowing back into Zane's coat. Dang it, I almost had him. I shifted my feet in the snow and looked over at the spot Bernie was interested in.

"You're sure that's the spot?" I asked the lump in Zane's coat.

A faint meow was my only response. I rolled my eyes and walked over, following his paw prints. Once I was in the center, I started kicking snow out of the way. Zane watched for a second before catching on.

"Great idea. It will save time if the area's cleared. I'll help."

"Well, if I'd remembered a shovel, we would already have the treasure, so I feel like I should do something."

"Hey, don't dig without me! You know I've always wanted to do this."

We spun and saw Logan trudging toward us. He had two shovels over his shoulder and was grinning like a kid.

"Hey, freckles! You've got some explaining to do before I bring out the big guns," Logan said, tossing down the shovels and flexing his arm.

"Oh no. I totally forgot the gun show was in town. How silly of me," I said, sticking out my tongue. "How'd you get here so quickly? And why didn't you bring three shovels? What am I supposed to dig with?"

"I was hanging out in my truck in Deadwood, waiting for you for the past two hours. You could've texted me sooner, you know. And you're not digging. That's what we're for. You can stand there and look pretty."

I narrowed my eyes and shook my head.

"Sorry, I should've called earlier. I'm more than happy to dig. Maybe you should stand here and look pretty."

"You know I'm kidding, little Red Riding Hood. Keep your shirt on," he said, rubbing his hands together before nodding at Zane. "Watch and see how it's done. Where do we start? What are we looking for, anyway?"

I slapped my hand over my mouth as I realized I hadn't really told Logan what we were looking for. It said everything about my cousin that he asked no questions and showed up just because I asked. He handed me a shovel while Zane found a safe place for Bernie to sit while we worked.

"Geez, I'm slipping. I forgot we hadn't talked about what's been going on. Start on that cleared spot, and I'll talk while you dig."

Logan made a face before hitting his shovel into the hard dirt.

"You couldn't have picked a better time to do this, you know? Why are we digging now instead of when it's nice and warm and the ground is soft?"

"Because we're looking for gold."

Logan's jaw dropped open, and the shovel he was holding fell to the ground.

"What?"

"Oh. Um. I might have forgotten to mention that the mine's payroll was in gold. Five hundred ounces."

"What? Five hundred ounces of gold? Do you realize how much that's worth?" Zane asked, letting out a whistle.

"I don't know? Maybe a hundred thousand?"

"Try a million, Brynnie," Logan said, his face white.

"You're kidding. What is there, like some secret man thing where you both know the price of gold and I don't?"

Logan snorted and looked at the ground I'd cleared, shaking his head.

"I just pay attention to the markets. You're sure about this?"

"Well, I guess I don't know if it's all here, but there were a bunch of saddlebags in my dream, and I'm pretty sure they held most, if not all, of the stolen payroll."

"Dream? Brynn, you've got a lot of explaining to do."

Logan and Zane exchanged a glance as Zane picked up his shovel.

"Like I said, you dig; I'll talk. I can spell you when you get tired."

"For that much money, you can talk all day, and I'll dig until I pass out," Logan said, shoving the head of the shovel into the ground with all his might. "You're sure this is the right spot?"

"Just dig."

I spent the next twenty minutes bringing Logan up to speed. Both men had stripped off their coats as they worked, and I hung them on some nearby branches. They took turns digging until the hole in front of me was about two feet deep.

"How much further?"

I peered into it and shrugged.

"I'm not sure. It looked really deep in my dream, but it's hard to tell. I think you're close, though."

"Very close," Bernie said, hopping down from his rock to join us. "Keep going, but be careful. Gold is soft, and those saddlebags probably are rotten."

I quickly translated for my cousin and Zane. They exchanged another look.

"You're sure we're in the right spot?"

"I'm sure."

As I spoke, a qualm of doubt wavered in my stomach, but I smiled anyway. Bernie said to trust him, and I did. Completely.

"So, what are we going to do with the gold when we find it? Split it three ways? Technically, since you didn't dig, Brynn, I'm not sure you should get a full share. You can call it a wedding present for me."

"Nice try, Logan. We're not keeping the money."

Zane kept digging, but my cousin came to a halt, giving me a look filled to the brim with disbelief.

"What now?"

"We can't keep it, Logan. Number one, we need to use it to trap the imp. After that, I think we should find the family who owned the mine and turn it in. It's not our money. If anything, it should go to the miners who weren't paid."

"How is it going to trap the imp?"

"I think, and Bernie thinks, Lame Jim is tied to this treasure. He sold his soul to a demon for this money. After the second hanging, they somehow merged. It's not a game, Logan. If there was ever such a thing as blood money, this is it. You don't want it. Not really. It's not worth the cost."

My cousin shook his head, but he picked up the shovel again and kept digging. He tossed a pile of dirt to the side and wiped his forehead while Zane carefully poked around the hole.

"Wait. I think I feel something," Zane said, his eyes bright as he looked at me.

I rushed forward, sending some dirt piled by the hole back in.

"Hey!" Logan said, holding out his hand.

"Sorry! I got excited. What's in there?"

Zane dropped to his knees and used his hands to clear away the dirt at the bottom of the hole. A piece of worn leather came away in his hand. He grinned as he held it up to me.

"You were right."

"Thanks," Bernie said, sniffing. "You don't need to sound so surprised."

Logan knelt by the hole and joined Zane in clearing away the dirt. Carefully, he pulled out another piece of leather.

"I can't believe it. My first buried treasure. Brynn, you need to film this."

"Oh, good idea," I said, rummaging in my pocket for my phone. "This is so exciting."

I hopped in place, sending a little more dirt into the hole. I hit the record button on my camera app just in time to catch Logan's dirty look as he smoothed away the dirt I'd kicked into the bottom of the hole.

"Seriously, you need to quit that."

I ignored my cousin and leaned down to get a better look. The weak sunlight glinted off something at the bottom. Our mouths fell open as Zane brushed away the remaining dirt, revealing a gold bar. Logan let out a cheer that echoed through the woods, startling a flock of birds. We danced around the hole, shouting nonsense. We'd found it. Bernie joined in, letting out a wail that made the hair on the back of my neck stand up. As difficult as uncovering the treasure had been, this was the simple part. The hard part was yet to come. I swallowed and pulled myself together. We were just getting started.

15

I raised my hands to the heat vents in Zane's Jeep as we pulled away from where we'd parked off the road. Bernie curled in my lap, tucking his tail over his nose. Zane's cheeks were flushed from the cold, and he was still grinning like a kid.

I glanced over my shoulder into the backseat, where five hundred ounces of gold bounced a little in Logan's donated tool bag as Zane took a corner.

"Careful."

"I'll slow down. I can't believe we have a million dollars in gold in the backseat of my car."

"You're not the only one. I'm glad Logan could spare that bag. It would be worse packing all of that in our pockets. Geez, I didn't even think to bring a container. I'm slipping."

I looked down at my cat, fully expecting a witty agreement, but he was silent. That was a first.

"You've had a lot going on. I didn't bring anything either. Heck, we weren't sure we'd find anything."

"I told you you can trust me," Bernie said, cracking open an eye.

There was the snark I knew and loved. I stroked his head and chuckled.

"We know, bud. We know. Zane, do you think we're doing the right thing by taking this to Dave?"

Zane nodded and tucked his hair behind an ear.

"I do. Given its history, I think this gold needs to be under lock and key until we're ready to spring the trap."

"I'm not sure Logan agrees with us."

I looked over my shoulder and spotted my cousin still behind us. It had taken all of my powers to convince him the sheriff's office was the best place to keep the gold. I wasn't sure about the way he'd eyed it as we stacked it in the bag.

Zane looked in the rearview mirror for a second and nodded slowly.

"He didn't want to part with that last bar, did he?"

"I just hope there isn't some sort of spell attached to the gold. He hasn't been himself lately. He's a good man, though. He'd never steal."

As I said the words, I meant them, but that didn't mean a tiny part of me wasn't worried. I'd counted every bar as we took them out of the hole and then again as we loaded them into the bag.

"There's no spell on it," Bernie said, yawning widely. "I made sure of it. Logan's just dealing with some stuff. He won't take the gold."

"Like what?"

"I'm not going to divulge his secrets to you. You're nosy enough you'll be able to pry it out of him."

"Hey! I'm not nosy."

Bernie gave a kitty snort and settled back into position on my lap. Okay, I was a little nosy. I'd known Logan my entire life. This was the first time he'd hidden something from me.

"Don't stress yourself out worrying about Logan," Zane said, taking my hand. "You've got enough on your plate. When he's ready to tell you what's bothering him, he will."

"I guess. I still can't believe we found the treasure. Fifty gold bars. What was that worth back in the day?"

Zane cocked his head to the side for a second.

"I don't know. Maybe ten thousand dollars?"

"Wow. To think that many people died for a measly ten grand."

THE IMP AT THE ICE RINK

"Well, back then, that was a lot of money, Brynn."

I leaned forward and grabbed my phone, typing in a quick search. My eyebrows raised as it converted that amount into today's dollars.

"Oh. So, it was similar to three hundred thousand today. I get it."

"I can't even imagine. I bet the mine owners were furious that it was never found. Do you think we'll be able to track them down?"

"Dave will know. I hope he's still in his office," I said, glancing at the clock on the dash.

It was almost quitting time, and the sun was dipping below the hill as we got to Deadwood. I'd finally warmed up from our treasure hunt and wasn't looking forward to getting back out of the car.

"His truck's still out front. You know how he is."

"True. If there was ever anyone dedicated to his job, it's Dave."

We parked, and Logan pulled into the spot next to us, radio blasting. I glanced down at Bernie.

"Do you want to come inside with us? Dave doesn't mind if you do."

"No, I'll stay out here, if that's okay with you. I'm shot."

I held him as I got out and put him back down in my warm seat, where he curled into a tight ball. Zane left the motor running as he got out and grabbed the bag from the back seat.

"Zip that up, man," Logan said as he got out of his pickup. "We can't afford to let anyone know what we've got in there."

Zane hiked the bag up and held it while I zipped it shut. Zane's knuckles were white as he carried the bag across the street. We flanked him, and I resisted the urge to look back and forth. It's not like any of us were used to transporting a million dollars in gold. Logan's back was tense as he opened the door for us, scanning the street.

"Act natural," I said, as quietly as I could.

I nodded at the deputy behind the desk and walked forward.

"Can we talk to Dave?"

"Head on back. I think he might be napping, though, so fair warning, he might be cranky."

I snorted and waved before walking down the hall. Dave's feet were up on the desk as we walked in, and he had his hands crossed over his thin chest. If he had been asleep, he quickly realized we were there. His sharp eyes scanned the three of us before narrowing.

"What are you three up to? You look as guilty as kids who just robbed a cookie jar."

We all took a seat, and Logan prodded me in the ribs with a sharp elbow. So much for acting natural. I guess I was going to take the lead.

"So, do you remember we were talking about Lame Jim and the robbery the other day?"

"I'm old, not feeble, Brynn. Of course, I remember. What I don't know yet is why you three are looking at me like troubled teens. Spill it."

Zane huffed a laugh but cut it off as I glanced over at him. I couldn't fault him, though. We were acting weird. I needed to just lay it all out there.

"We found the treasure."

Dave levered himself upright and narrowed his eyes at me.

"So you're telling me you found the treasure that numerous detectives, search parties, and treasure hunters have been looking for over the past one hundred years?"

"That's exactly what I am saying. We brought it with us. That's why we're here."

"Brynn, for Pete's sake, just spit it out," Logan said. "This is why I'm always the talker of the family. This one here hems and haws until the cows come home."

"Hey!"

Dave rolled his eyes before focusing on me.

"I swear. You two haven't changed a bit. I'm not going to ask how you found it. I don't want to know. My question is, what are you going to do with it?"

"We were hoping you could help us with that."

I strained to pick up the tool bag. Zane leaned forward and supported it from underneath, lifting it onto Dave's desk with an audible thump.

"Hey, watch it. We don't want the bars scuffed," Logan said.

Dave's eyebrows went so far up they could have replaced his missing hairline. I nodded at him as he reached for the zipper. Slowly, he opened the bag and pulled the sides apart. His thin face flushed as he looked back at me.

"This is a fortune," he said, lifting the bag up slightly. "This has to be over thirty pounds. Why did you just put a bag with a million dollars of gold on my desk?"

"Seriously, what is with knowing the price of gold? Am I the only one who's completely in the dark? Anyway, we were hoping you could keep it safe until tomorrow. We're going to need it to trap the imp, but after that's done, I want it to go back to the rightful owner," I said. "I don't feel comfortable hiding this in my house."

Dave looked at me, not saying a word, for an uncomfortably long time. Well, at least it felt super uncomfortable. It probably wasn't that long.

"All right. I'll put it in the safe, and when this is done, we'll figure it out from there. I'm glad you brought this to me. I know you three are tight, but all it would take is the wrong person finding out about this, and you'd be in a world of danger, missy. Gold fever is a real thing. How are you going to use this to trap whatever it is you're trapping?"

I cocked my head to the side and rubbed a finger on the arm of the chair.

"Honestly? I'm not sure, but we'll figure it out. I'm just relieved you'll help us."

"You did the right thing. I know it can't be easy for you to hand this over. I always knew you were good eggs, but this is above and beyond. A lot of people would have been tempted to keep it and never mention it, especially since you found the whole lot buried together. I would've thought Lame Jim would've split it up with his compadres."

Logan cleared his throat and stood, pushing his chair back.

"I need to get going. I've got to get up to that house and get a plan put together to keep the renovation going."

"We already started demolition in the kitchen," I said, standing. "But there's plenty left to do."

He tossed me a brief smile before heading out of Dave's office. I glanced at Zane and shook my head.

"He okay?" Dave asked, picking up the bag with a grunt. "Holy smokes, this is heavy."

"I think so. Well, I hope so."

"You'll figure it out. You always do. Are we still on for three at the saloon?"

"As far as I know. We'll be early to make sure we've got all our ducks in a row. I need to do a little more research, but it seems like everything is coming together."

"You know more about this than I do, but whatever you need, I'll be there. I'm going to put this in the safe. See you two later."

He plopped his cowboy hat on his head and gave us a nod before walking out of his office. Zane took my hand as we walked back to the front.

"What do we do now?"

I shook my head and braced myself as we walked back into the cold.

"I wish I knew. Maybe Bernie will have some ideas."

"Let's run to the store and pick up a few things. I can make dinner while you're researching, and then we can talk it through."

I leaned against his arm for a second before we split up to get into the Jeep. Having Zane around was the best thing that ever happened to me. In the midst of chaos, he was my rock. And it didn't hurt that he loved to cook. I hopped in and peeked into the backseat, where Bernie had curled up. His ears twitched as we headed to the store. We had a little more than twenty-four hours left before I would have to face down the imp. While I still wasn't sure what I needed to do, my friends and I would figure it out.

16

The next morning found me out of sorts and restless. My dreams had been shapeless, but I couldn't shake the feeling of dread that crept around the edges of my soul, refusing to let go. Every time I closed my eyes, the image of Lame Jim's strange pupils haunted me. I blew out a deep breath and paced around my living room.

"Do you need to get outside or something? You're driving me nuts with this pacing. Zane's patience has even worn thin."

I flopped dramatically on the couch next to Bernie and pouted. He wasn't wrong. Zane, sensing my mood, had left an hour ago to get some work done. I should have been doing something. I tried reading more about Lame Jim, but after the fifth time of repeating the same paragraph, I'd given up. I could typically focus on a task, but today? Today I felt like I was coming apart at the seams. Nothing was working.

"I know. I'm sorry. I just can't keep my mind focused. How are we going to win this battle? I've never banished a demon, big or small. What if I fail? What if I can't do it right? What will happen to the town?"

"There are a lot of what-ifs rattling around in that head of yours. I think we need to visit Mallory. She'll help ground you."

I sat straight up on the couch.

"That's a great idea."

"I'm full of them."

I leaned over and planted a loud kiss on his little forehead.

"You're full of something. I'll give you that. Want to tag along?"

"As much as I wouldn't mind napping without distraction, I'll come with. You might need me."

I sprang off the couch and paused.

"What do you mean by that?"

"Well, you're the key component for tonight's ritual. I'm pretty sure the imp knows this. If they take you out, no ritual."

He sauntered toward the door, tail waving, as though he hadn't just dropped a verbal atomic bomb.

"Hey, wait. What do you mean?"

Bernie picked a great time to go silent as he loaded himself into his bag. I shook my head and zipped him in. As if I didn't have enough to worry about. I pulled on my coat and grabbed my tote bag. Maybe Mallory would have some words of wisdom to put my mind at ease.

The drive to Deadwood was quick, but as I pulled into town, enormous detour signs blocked my usual way in. I frowned as I followed the signs. Bernie sat bolt upright in his bag.

"Let me out."

"What? Why?"

"Let me out of this bag. Now."

I used one hand to free him and watched out of the corner of my eye as he placed his little paws on the dash, standing on his back legs.

"What's wrong?"

"This detour isn't good. You know where we're going?"

I thought about it for a second before blanching. The road we were now on passed the square with the ice rink. Surely that couldn't be possible. Right?

"It's got to be a coincidence. There's no way."

Bernie shot me a look.

"Right. How many actual coincidences do we run into?"

"Um. A few?"

"Name one."

I tapped my fingers on the steering wheel as traffic started again. Yeah, coincidences were pretty rare lately. I took a deep breath and focused on the road.

"There isn't another way through town. The other road is one-way, and we're going the wrong way. We've got no choice. It's the rink or turn around and go back the long way. It could take over an hour to do that. What should I do?"

"Don't worry. I've got you. Put your shield up."

"Easy for you to say. I'm still not very good at it."

We turned the corner and started down the road past the square. I did my best to slow my heart rate and imagine a brick wall in my head protecting my thoughts. The line of cars crept forward, and I kept my eyes straight ahead. While I doubted the imp would appear in broad daylight, I wouldn't risk it.

Bernie sat next to me, eyes closed, as we approached the rink. A faint ache in my shoulder made me loosen my grip on the steering wheel.

"Fight it, Brynn."

I ground my teeth together and redoubled my efforts to protect my mind. Traffic started moving faster, and finally, we passed the rink. My breath came out in a shudder, and I glanced over at Bernie.

"You okay, bud?"

His shoulders slumped as he sank down onto the seat. Whatever he'd done, he looked exhausted.

"I'm fine. I need some food, though."

"Say no more. We'll hit up a drive-through before we go to Mallory's."

I zeroed in on the bagel hut up ahead and turned off the main road. Perfect. I ordered a coffee with a breakfast bagel topped with eggs and bacon and drummed my fingers on the steering wheel while I waited. The girl in the window handed over the food, and I didn't even wait to pull ahead to unwrap the bagel and place it on the seat next to my cat.

Bernie's eyes gleamed before he started scarfing down eggs and bacon. My coffee wasn't even cool enough to drink by the time he'd polished off the toppings.

"You can have the bagel."

"Er, thanks, but I'll pass."

I love my cat, but the thought of eating a bagel topped with cat slobber was low on my list. My stomach was so twisted in knots that, for once, food didn't even sound good.

He let out a sigh and curled back up in his bag, content. I took a sip of coffee while I waited for the traffic light to change. We only had two lights in town, and I was stuck behind one of them. The warm hazelnut flavor brightened my mood. Ah, that was better.

By the time I got to Mallory's shop, I was a lot less frazzled. I parked and checked on my cat.

"Do you want to hang out here?"

"No. I'll go in with you."

He hopped out of his bag and dove into my lap. Okay, then. I guess I was carrying him. I got out and walked up to the door, stopping short when I noticed the closed sign.

"Oh, no. I guess I should've called."

"She's here. Knock."

I moved him around in my arms to free up a hand and rapped on the glass. Everything inside was dark, but I spotted movement.

"Hey, you were right."

Bernie muttered under his breath, but I ignored it. I already knew what he was saying. Mallory's face was drawn, but she gave me a shaky smile as she opened the door.

"I had a feeling you'd be coming today. How are you holding up?"

Bernie hopped down and circled Mallory as I took one of her arms.

"Are you okay? You look..."

"I know. I can't sleep. Every time I do, I see these horrible eyes. The pupils are full of flame. It's awful."

I took a step back.

"Seriously? That's how I saw Lame Jim in my dream."

"Dream?"

I nodded and looped my arm through hers.

"We need to talk. A lot has been going on."

She led me into the back room of her shop, and I looked around, surprised. It wasn't what I expected from my bohemian friend. The regular part of the shop was brightly colored and full of art. This space was stark white with industrial tables. A pile of herbs sat on a table next to what looked like an ancient mortar and pestle.

"Welcome to my lab," she said, walking over to the table. "I'm working on a new blend of herbs that I think will help tonight. I just wish it would help me sleep."

I spun around, gaping at everything. Bernie, who'd never met a table he hadn't jumped on, sat at my feet, respecting her space. She wasn't kidding when she said it was a lab.

"This is mind-blowing. I'd never know this was back here. Is this where you prepare everything you sell?"

Mallory flashed a smile over her shoulder.

"It is. I special-ordered the tables when I opened the store. They weren't cheap, but I love this space. I can focus here. Well, usually. Not so much today."

"I've been the same way."

"You mentioned a dream?"

"Sorry. I got distracted. You'll never believe what's happened."

I talked while she worked. I wasn't sure what they were, but the smell was comforting. By the time I was done wrapping up our adventure from the day before, I felt much calmer.

"Wow. You found the gold? That's incredible! That's what we needed for the trap. I was looking through my jewelry for some gold, but I have nothing pure enough. And you deliver five hundred ounces of it. Amazing."

"So, how is this going to work?"

Mallory brushed off her hands and turned to me, stretching out her back with a groan.

"I'm not sure what Ned has planned, but as soon as I'm done with these, we'll have the protection herbs we need. We'll use the gold to draw the imp out from his place of power. Once we have that, you'll do your thing and send him back whence he came."

It sounded simple, but something told me it would be anything but. I nodded and tried to smile.

"Dave will be there and Zane, too. I don't know if they can help, but they'll do their best."

"It's a good thing I'm making enough of this mix for everyone. Where do you want to meet? We should probably prepare beforehand."

"You know where I live, right? Why don't you come to my house when you're done, and we'll order a pizza?"

"Deal. One veggie pizza for me, please. I don't know if I'll be able to eat, but I'll try."

I put my hand over my stomach and grimaced.

"Same. It's worth a try, though. I've never turned down pizza. Is there anything I can help with? You're doing so much by yourself. I feel like I'm just drifting about, letting everyone else do the heavy lifting."

Mallory walked over and gave me a quick hug.

"Says the woman who found the treasure no one else could. You'll play the most important role. If you can, try to rest. You'll need all your strength for tonight."

"I don't think that's going to happen, but I'll try. See you soon."

"Take the back way to Brynn's house," Bernie said, bumping against Mallory's leg.

"Why?"

I slapped my hand to my head.

"That's right. The detour. If you go the usual way, you'll have to drive right past the rink. We just came that way, and it was not fun. Here, I'll show you a different way to get to Gilded City."

I pulled out my phone and showed her the long way. She ran her fingers through her lilac hair and nodded.

"It will add a bunch of travel time, especially tonight. He knows we're moving on him. I wish there was a way to get the detour rerouted."

"You know what? I'll call Dave. Maybe he can help us out. Great idea!"

She shrugged and handed my phone back.

"It was your idea, silly. Let me know which way to take. I'd better get back to work."

Bernie led the way to the door while I dialed Dave's number. It took a few rings, but he answered as we walked outside.

"Yeah?"

"Happy day to you, too, Dave."

"Sorry, it's been one of those days. What's up?"

"You know the detour going through town?"

"That's where I am right now. There's just been an accident."

My heart sank, and I stopped at my car.

"Oh, no. Was anyone hurt?"

"Minor injuries. Why did you want to know about the detour?"

"I think it's a fake. Don't ask me how, but we need to get it rerouted. The imp knows its time is short. Whatever havoc it can wreak will only strengthen it. When London shut the rink down, it ran out of victims. I don't know how it influenced the detour, but it needs to be changed."

Dave was quiet, but I could feel the gears in his head working. He barked out a sharp cuss and sighed.

"I'll figure it out. I'll call when it's done."

"Thanks, Dave."

I breathed a sigh of relief and ended the call. This day was just getting stranger. While it wouldn't make my drive home any shorter, at least I knew Dave would do his best to ensure the detour was changed. I opened the door, and Bernie hopped in, snuggling into the passenger seat.

"Is everyone okay?"

"He said minor injuries. Thankfully. I just don't understand."

"Demons excel at the power of suggestion. My money's on

someone waking up with the idea they needed to reroute traffic. We'll fight him, Brynn. We'll win. Don't let this derail you."

"Well, it's going to derail our trip home. I should text Zane and let him know what's going on. I don't want him anywhere near that place."

I fired off a quick text before starting my car and heading out. At least the long way was a scenic drive. I'd have plenty to look at on my way home. And plenty of time to think.

17

Considering that my afternoon had moved like molasses, now that our showdown was just an hour away, it felt as though we were running out of time. I kept checking my watch as Zane drove down the twisting highway. Mallory leaned forward from the backseat and patted my arm.

"It's going to be fine. We're as prepared as we're going to be."

I answered with a weak smile and looked out the window, holding Bernie a little closer to my chest. I wanted to believe it. I truly did. Exhaustion crept over me, warring with the amped-up feeling coursing through my chest. I hadn't been able to nap, and even though pizza was one of my favorite things on earth, I'd barely choked down a slice. I felt Zane's hand close around mine in the dark.

"Let's go over the plan one more time. It will help the rest of the drive go faster."

"Okay. We're going to meet Dave and get the gold. We'll give him his packet of herbs and make sure he parks far enough away. He won't be injured if anything goes sideways. From there, we'll find Ned and approach the rink together. Zane, I think you should hang back with Dave."

"Not going to happen."

The dash lights lit up his face enough that I could see him shaking his head.

"But..."

"We're a team, Brynn. I'm not leaving your side. That's non-negotiable. While you're getting Ned, I'm going to set up my camera. I might see something on it you can't."

His special camera had captured ghosts in the past, but I wasn't sure if an imp would show up on the screen.

"He's smart," Bernie said, stretching from his spot on my lap. "While you're doing all of that, I'm going to get into position. Remember, Brynn, you've got to shield."

The amount of things I needed to do hung over me like an extra-heavy sword. I wasn't sure how this was all going to work, but I'd do whatever it took to banish this imp and Lame Jim. I could only hope it would be enough.

All the detour signs were gone, and Zane turned down a side street so we wouldn't pass the rink. I'm sure the imp knew something was up, but it needed no more advance notice. We pulled into the bank parking lot near the square, and Zane cut the engine.

"You've got your packets, right?" Mallory asked, rustling around in the backseat.

I patted the square mesh bag in my front pocket and nodded.

"Right here. Zane?"

"Got it."

Mallory had made a small sachet to go around Bernie's neck, tied with a purple ribbon, and he looked adorable. I wouldn't tell him that, especially since he'd initially fought wearing it. I patted his head and reached for the door handle.

"Everyone ready?"

"Let's do this," Bernie said, hopping out of my lap and streaking into the distance, his black fur blending into the night.

I stood for a second, trying to pick him out.

"He'll be okay, Brynn. You know he's smart."

"I know. If something happened to him, though, I'd never forgive myself."

Mallory joined us and folded her arms across her chest.

"Lead the way. I'm uncertain where Dave wanted to meet."

I started walking as they fell in next to me. I turned down a side street, brightening when I saw Dave's pickup parked with the lights off. His window was down, and I could smell the coffee he'd just poured from his ancient thermos.

"Glad you could make it," I said as we approached.

Dave harrumphed a hello and tilted his head toward Mallory.

"Evening, Miss Mallory. It's good to see you."

"You too, Sheriff."

"Alright, kids. I'm here, and I brought the gold. What do we do now?"

He took a loud sip of his coffee and smacked his lips before getting out of his truck. He'd swapped out his usual uniform for an all-black outfit. I smiled and shook my head.

"We'll need you as backup. I don't know what's going to happen, but I don't want you in the line of fire, so to speak," I said before glancing at Zane. "If something, well, happens, could you call Logan?"

"Logan's already here," a voice echoed down the empty street. "Did you really think I'd let you go into this alone?"

I swore under my breath and turned to see my cousin approaching. Luckily, he'd left Kelsie at home.

"I'm not alone. Zane, Mallory, and Dave are here. Logan, you shouldn't be here."

"Whatever, firecracker. Let's get this show on the road. If we've got to give away all this gold, I need to be a part of this."

He smiled at Mallory before punching Zane playfully on the shoulder. Zane raised an eyebrow and went back to looking at his camera.

"I've got it all set up. I'm going to position myself in the alley next to the rink until you've got Ned. Logan can help."

"What do I need to do with the gold?" Dave asked.

Logan eyed the toolbag Dave was holding and raised a hand.

"I'll take that. You said you needed it for the trap, right? We'll be right next to the rink, and you won't have to lug it around town. We'll go the back way so we won't be spotted."

I searched my cousin's face in the dark and liked what I saw. I nodded.

"Okay. Logan, you're in charge of the gold. Zane, you're in charge of the camera. Dave, you'll be in reserve. We'll go find Ned. Keep an eye out for Bernie. I don't know where he went."

Everyone went their way as I walked forward, Mallory on my heels. I turned onto the main road and searched for Ned. Following my gut instinct, I went to the original location of the saloon and waited, looking up and down the street.

"Took you long enough, missy."

I jumped out of my skin and spun around to see Ned snickering in the doorway.

"What the heck? You nearly gave me a heart attack. Usually, you have a little more fanfare to announce your arrival."

I put my hand on my chest to slow my skittering heart. Ned chuckled and tipped his hat to Mallory.

"Glad you're here, too. I'm saving up my energy. Let's go. I wanna see this newfangled ice rink."

Mallory shrugged, and I spun on my heel, heading toward the rink. A twinge shot through my shoulder, and I stopped, gasping for breath. Right. I needed a shield. I imagined a wall in my mind and moved forward. Ned glided alongside, looking at the businesses.

"You'll have to tell me what happened to the saloon. The sign said it was the Wild Bill Bar."

"It moved to a new spot on Main Street. I had a feeling you'd go to where it used to be."

"Hmph. Makes little sense to me. Why'd they move it?"

"Long story, Ned. I'll tell you later."

"Psst. Over here."

My head whipped to the side, and I quickly relaxed as I saw Zane and Logan at the mouth of the alley. I really could have done without all these shocks to my system. By the time I made it to the rink, I was going to be a mess. Okay, I was already a mess.

THE IMP AT THE ICE RINK

I grabbed the tool bag, grunting as I gave Logan a nod. Zane fell in next to me, holding his camera up.

"I'm already picking up an interesting heat signature in that direction," he said, pointing toward the rink. "It's like nothing I've seen before. It's this massive red blob."

Ned drifted closer, and I motioned for Zane to lower the camera so Ned could see it.

"Well, I'll be tarred and feathered. Look at that. How does that thing work?"

"Later, Ned. Let's get this over with."

We approached the rink and stood there, looking at it under the glow of the streetlights. Logan walked forward a little, but Mallory darted to stop him.

"Oh, I almost forgot. Here, Logan, you need this," Mallory said, pressing his packet of herbs into his hand.

Logan looked at it for a second before glancing at me. I nodded, and he shoved it into his pocket. Even though the night was cold, sweat dripped down my back as I edged closer to the rink and dropped the bag.

"What's in there?" Ned asked, circling it.

"The gold. Move aside, Ned; it's part of our trap. I don't know how it's going to work, but I don't want you to get caught up in it."

Ned's eyes gleamed in the dark, but he fell back, sniffing the air.

"That's pure gold you've got there, missy. I know that smell."

A horrible shriek split the air, and my blood ran cold. It was showtime. A black shape detached from a building and moved like a streak of lightning toward me, skidding to a stop in the middle of the street. My heart nearly came out of my chest until I realized it was my cat.

"Stop. Everyone but Brynn and Ned needs to move back. You two, join me."

I glanced at Zane, and the look in his eyes nearly dropped me to my knees. He was terrified at the thought of me approaching the imp without him. Logan grabbed his shoulder and leaned close, whispering something I couldn't hear. I smiled and winked before turning back and walking forward, glad my cousin showed up. If nothing else, he would keep Zane from doing something rash.

"Alright, girly. It's just you, me, and the cat. Let's see what this imp's made of."

"Brynn! Wait."

I stopped and looked at Mallory.

"What?"

"You can do this. Cast all doubt aside. You need to know you are surrounded by more help than you can ever imagine."

"I hope you're right. Make sure they're okay. Please."

She nodded and stepped in front of the guys. Buoyed by her words and knowing she'd protect Logan and Zane, I walked forward again until I reached Bernie, who was sitting next to the bag.

"Ready?"

"As ready as I'm going to be. What do we need to do?"

"Just wait."

Ned twirled around the bag of gold before coming to a stop in the middle of the street and bellowing.

"Come on out, you yellow-bellied, lily-livered bottom feeder. I know you're here! I can smell your fear."

Well, that was one way to get the imp and Lame Jim out of hiding. I might have worded things a little differently, but Ned looked like he was having the time of his afterlife.

A deep, horrible laugh reverberated in my eardrums, chilling my blood. Mist filled the street, taking on a sickly orange glow, touched with red. I swallowed hard and marshaled every bit of inner strength I could find.

"Lame Jim, your time has come. Face your sentence and accept your destiny."

Bernie's voice sounded strange. Much deeper and louder than I ever would've thought possible. I glanced down in surprise and noticed he was lit with a pure white glow. He was the size of a mountain lion as he stepped in front of me.

"Bernie?"

He ignored me and gnashed his teeth against the mist. A squeal shot through the street, echoing off the buildings.

"You dare to tell me what to do, you puny thing. You have no power here."

The swirling mist coalesced into a form right in front of my cat, and my heart stopped beating for a split second. This creature was over twenty feet tall and loomed over us, faceless, with fangs that appeared to drip some terrible substance from its bottomless maw.

"Oh, knock it off, you two-bit charlatan. You don't scare us. Now go on and git. Your time here is long gone," Ned said, spitting onto the street.

"You dare to mock me? Who do you think you are?"

"I'm Ned Davis, an honest man, which is more than I can say about you. I know you're in there, Lame Jim. You're not fooling anyone with your dark arts."

The form seemed to inhale, sucking air out of the street like we were in a wind tunnel. Debris careened around us but bounced off right before it reached me. What the heck?

Bernie, still glowing, met my eyes and gave me a solemn nod. I guess it was my turn.

"Lame Jim and, uh, Mr. Imp, you don't belong here. You need to leave."

Yeah, it wasn't my best effort, but hey, I'm awful under pressure and not exactly used to dealing with demons. Especially when they're twenty feet tall and inhaling everything.

Its response was to unleash a laugh so loud I smacked my hands over my ears to block it out.

"Little girl, who do you think you are? Mere mortals and ghosts mean nothing to me. You have something of mine, and I will not be denied. I have waited too long for this. Hand over the gold!"

"No. No, we won't be doing that. You won't be hurting anyone else, either. I don't know what you are or how you two became fused together, but this is not your place. The people in this town will not live in fear. Not if I can help it."

Strength flooded into my soul, and I stood as tall as I could, glaring into the face of hell as it leaned closer to me. A horrible stench hit my nose, and my stomach roiled.

"Who are you?"

"Brynn Sullivan. Your worst nightmare."

I spread my arms wide and prayed for help. An idea formed in my head, and I smiled as everything became clear. Bernie's glow doubled in size, and warmth filled my heart. The familiar light I saw when I helped ghosts move on appeared, but this time, it was directly over me. Peace filled my soul as the light expanded to include Ned and Bernie.

Suddenly, the monster in front of us reared back, unleashing a fearful scream.

"No. No! I will not be denied. This wasn't part of my bargain!"

A grinding noise filled the street, and I resisted the urge to glance over my shoulder to make sure everyone we'd left behind was okay. Somehow, I knew I needed to keep my attention on the imp.

The light around Bernie doubled in size, and I blinked as I realized he was no longer alone. A pure white cat, even bigger than his current form, was standing next to him.

"Go. You are finished," the white cat said, her voice as soft as tinkling bells.

Somehow, the street cracked open in front of us. Ned hooted and hollered, spinning around in glee as the monster was pulled below us, its mist-like hands grabbing the surrounding buildings. Bricks crumbled, and I swallowed hard.

"Keep it up, Brynn," Bernie said. "Don't stop."

I wasn't sure what I was doing, but I lifted my arms higher and closed my eyes. Tortured screams drowned out the sound of my breath, leaving an echo in my head that I was sure would never leave. A sonic blast knocked me off my feet, and I hit the pavement as the windows next to me exploded. Suddenly, a hush filled the air. I cracked open one eye and then the other, crawling up on my elbows.

Ned was dancing a jig over the street that somehow was whole again, singing a nonsensical song. I snorted and turned my attention to the white cat standing next to Bernie. They had returned to normal cat size and were deep in conversation.

I struggled to my feet and dusted off my jeans, looking around the street, convinced I'd imagined everything. The broken glass in the surrounding buildings and the bricks littering the street confirmed it hadn't been a dream.

"Brynn, it's a pleasure to meet you," the white cat said, turning to face me. "We weren't sure you had it in you, but we're pleasantly surprised."

I felt like a grimy peasant facing a queen. Her delicate paws seemed to float over the pavement as she approached. What was going on?

"Uh... thank you?"

Her musical laugh tinkled as Bernie joined her.

"Bernard was right about you. We weren't pleased when you discovered how to communicate with each other," she said, shooting a glacial look at Ned. "But we can see how beneficial it was."

Ned floated closer and frowned down at the two cats.

"You're darn tootin' it was beneficial, Miss Fancy Paws. This here girl is pure of heart. Anyone can see that. Now, if you'll excuse me, I'm a busy man."

Ned winked at me, giving his signature lopsided grin before vanishing. Dang it. I didn't have time to thank him. The white cat rose and circled Bernie.

"Bernard, you'll be happy to know your cousin Millicent has been chosen for a new assignment. Until we meet again."

She nodded regally and winked out of sight. I put my hands on my hips and looked down at my cat.

"You've got some explaining to do. Who was that cat?"

"Brynn? Is it over? Are you hurt?"

I glanced down the street as Zane jogged closer, arms wide. I gave Bernie a look that promised an interrogation as soon as we were alone. He gave a kitty shrug and jogged toward the bag of gold in the street. Somehow, it hadn't been sucked into the depths. I shook my head, not wanting to think about where Lame Jim and the imp ended up. It would surely feature in my nightmares later. Right now, I just wanted to feel Zane's powerful arms around me.

18

I'd like to say everything went back to normal, but my ability to be normal is deeply in question. The streets were still dark when Dave joined us, shaking his head as he aimed his flashlight at the mess left behind.

"We'll have to get someone here to clean all this up before the sun comes up. Do I even want to know what happened?"

I peeked at Dave from where I'd sequestered myself under Zane's arm and shrugged.

"Probably not. I don't know if I'll ever be able to forget it. Sometimes, it's better not knowing."

"Take her word for it, Dave. I only saw part of it. I'm not sure I'm ready to review the footage from my camera," Zane said. "But I heard it all. I'm just glad this isn't a residential area."

He looked up at the buildings and shuddered. The damage wasn't too extensive, but it was going to be interesting coming up with an explanation of how windows were shattered and enormous chunks of brick ended up in the middle of the street, rather than on the buildings where they belonged.

"Earthquake," Dave said, rubbing his chin. "A tremor came

through. That's the only way to explain this. I'm on it. I'll have the city send their team. I know Josh. He'll be grateful for the overtime."

I opened my mouth to respond but surprised myself by yawning instead. I heard Mallory's soft voice from behind me.

"I knew you could do it. It took everything you had. You must be exhausted."

I flashed a smile at her and nodded.

"I feel boneless. And starved. Anyone want to come back to my place, I mean, our place, and have some pizza?" I asked, looking up at Zane. "We've got a ton of leftovers from earlier."

Logan shook his head and stuck his hands in his pockets.

"Nah, but thanks. I'll head home."

I called to my cousin as he slouched away into the darkness of the street, but he raised a hand in a wave, refusing to turn around. What the heck? I turned toward Zane, pleading with my eyes.

"Let him go, Brynn. Whatever is on his mind, he's not ready to share it yet. When he is, he'll come to you. That's how he's wired. Until then, you need to give him some space."

"That's easy for you to say."

I frowned and focused back on Dave.

"Do you think people will buy the earthquake story?"

"I think it's a little easier to swallow than a demon ransacking downtown, don't you?"

"Good point. Okay, earthquake it is. Do you need us to file a report or anything?"

Dave shrugged and waved me off.

"It's better if you're not connected to this. I can say I noticed it while I was doing my rounds. You should go home, Brynn."

"What about the gold?" I asked, turning to look at where the bag was still lying in the street.

"I'll put it in my safe and we'll deal with it later. Go home and get some rest."

Well, when he put it like that, who was I to argue? I yawned again and leaned heavily on Zane as Dave walked toward the gold, talking into his cell phone.

"Mallory, do you want to stay the night with us? I don't want you to have to drive home this late. Or, I guess I should say this early."

"Would you mind dropping me at home? I want to be among familiar things tonight. It's a lot to process."

"Sure. We'll bring your car to you tomorrow."

"I appreciate it. I'm sorry to be a party pooper, but I need to cleanse myself of that energy I felt. I'd recommend burning some sage in your house before you go to sleep, Brynn."

I didn't think I had any sage, but after looking at her face and seeing how exhausted she looked, I figured now wasn't the time to bring it up. I waved at Dave before following Zane back to his Jeep. Bernie trudged along next to us. He looked so small and delicate as he walked. I couldn't believe that just minutes ago he'd seemed so big. I stopped and scooped him up, cradling him in my arms.

"You okay, bud?"

He buried his head under my chin, and his purrs made me smile as I started walking again. There was no way I was letting him off the hook about what I'd seen, but right now, it was fine to pretend he was just a normal cat, comforting his owner. We climbed into the Jeep, and Zane drove to Mallory's shop. She patted my shoulder before hopping out and disappearing inside. We waited until a light came on in the small apartment above her shop before driving away.

"Are you sure you're okay?" Zane asked, glancing over at me as he pulled onto the highway.

"I'm fine. Tired, but fine. When you were watching, did you see Bernie?"

Zane was quiet for a second, and I looked over to catch his expression, lit by the lights on the dash.

"I saw a bright light, but that's all. For a second, I thought I heard him, but my mind might have been playing tricks on me. Why?"

I looked down at Bernie snoozing in my lap.

"He grew somehow while we were confronting the imp. He was almost the size of a mountain lion. I was hoping you saw it too. Did you see another cat? Maybe I imagined the whole thing."

Zane huffed a sharp laugh and took my hand.

"I didn't see a second cat. Just a huge, terrifying shape that I thought would crush you. If these past few months have taught me anything, it's that you're hardly fanciful. If you saw something, it was there."

I nodded and looked out the window, catching my reflection. My hair was straggling out of my ponytail, but considering I'd just faced off against a demon, things could definitely be worse. I know it was a minor demon, but still.

As soon as my house came into view, a warm feeling of contentment spread through my bones. A few short months ago, it had been my refuge. My special little house that I'd renovated myself. Now? Now it was becoming something new. A place I would share with Zane as our relationship grew.

"I love your smile."

I turned my head back to Zane and found him watching me with a curious expression on his face, his heart in his eyes.

"I love yours, too."

"What were you thinking just now?"

I shrugged and slid out of my seat, gripping Bernie so I didn't dump him into the snowdrift next to Zane's Jeep.

"A lot of things. Mainly how happy I am that we're home. Our home."

Zane grinned as he walked around the front of his car and joined us.

"I do like the sound of that. It's a special place, Brynn. And you're a special woman."

My heart felt like it would burst as we walked inside. Bernie gave a happy chirp and launched himself out of my arms, heading right to the kitchen. I shook my head as I followed him. He'd more than earned a special treat.

Zane opened the fridge and put the pizza on plates while I dished up some salmon for Bernie. Nothing but the best for my little cat. And yes, I was going to save him some cheese from my pizza.

I leaned against the counter, watching Bernie dig into his food with abandon, and barely heard the beep of the microwave signaling that the pizza was ready. I stared at the plate Zane handed me as a wave of exhaustion crashed into my chest.

Was I actually too tired to eat? I took my plate over to the table and put it down, spotting a wrapped bundle and a note.

"Just some sage for your home. Light the end of the smudging stick and walk around your house before you go to sleep. Love, Mallory."

"She thinks of everything, doesn't she?" I asked, turning to look at Zane as he joined me with his plate.

"Who?"

"Mallory. She left us some sage. I hope I have the energy to burn it before bed."

He kissed me on the top of the head as he took a seat next to me.

"I'll do it. I can't say I've ever saged a place before, but you know what? Considering what goes on in our lives, it's probably an excellent skill to learn."

I picked up a slice of pizza and took a small bite as my appetite came roaring back. Whew, I was worried I might be sick. We were silent as we ate our early breakfast. By the time I was done, I felt stronger, but my feet didn't want to move.

"I've got dishes," Zane said, stacking my plate on his. "Just hang out and decompress."

Yep, I'm a lucky woman. Bernie hopped onto the table and rubbed his head against my arm.

"He's a wonderful addition to our team."

He laid out on the table and blinked his green eyes at me. I picked up the morsel of cheese I'd saved for him and handed it over.

"Here you go, bud. I didn't forget you. And yes, Zane is amazing."

He bolted down the cheese and licked his muzzle.

"I'm so proud of you and the woman you're becoming."

His rare praise brought tears to my eyes. Even though we'd only been able to communicate for a few months, Bernie had been a part of my life since I was three years old. I wiped the tears away as Zane came back to the table.

"Are you okay?"

"Yes," I said, sniffling. "Bernie just said the sweetest thing to me."

"Don't get all weird," Bernie said, placing a paw on my arm. "You've still got a lot to learn."

There he was. My beautiful, snarky cat. Or should I say, my snarky guardian? I raised an eyebrow as Zane picked up the sage and read the note.

"Okay, so I just light it and walk around? Do I need to say a prayer or anything?" Zane asked, looking between us.

I shrugged and looked at Bernie.

"Keep your intention of cleansing the house of any negativity as you go room by room. Prayers never hurt, either."

I passed along the instructions. Zane nodded before walking into the kitchen and rummaging through my junk drawer. He beamed as he held up a lighter.

"I'll start in the back and work my way back here."

I waited until Zane left the room before drumming my fingers on the table and giving Bernie our special look.

"What?"

"Spill it. Who was the white cat? Do you have a cousin? What exactly is a guardian?"

"You always have had an excellent memory," Bernie said, shifting a little before letting out a sigh. "I suppose there's no way of keeping it from you any longer. You've seen too much."

"As long as you don't have to kill me after," I said, teasing him as I stroked his head.

He fixed me with a serious look, and I took my hand away.

"You know about angels, right?"

I nodded and ran my fingers through my hair, taking out my hair tie.

"Well, I guess so. My mom always talked about them when I was little. I've never seen one, but I believe in them. Or the concept, at least."

"Angels are real. Very real. But there are only so many to go around. Sometimes, they need a little help. That's where we come in."

"The guardians?"

"That's the name that some people give us. It stuck through the ages. Anyway, if you'd stop interrupting me, I could probably tell the story better."

I rolled my eyes and waved my hand.

"Proceed."

He licked the fur of his ruff and shifted again.

"I can't believe I'm telling you everything. Okay, so there are guardians, typically animals, who are assigned to specific people. We watch over them and guide them through difficult times."

"Are all guardians cats?"

"Not all. There are dogs who are brought in to assist when it's necessary."

"So when you hear about a cat or a dog who saves someone's life, they're guardians?" I asked, staring at him in awe.

He nodded and gave his usual kitty shrug.

"It's not always about the heroics, though. Most of the time, it's small stuff. Many times, the human may not even realize they've been helped. We're supposed to be incognito."

"Who's the white cat? What did she mean by your cousin was assigned to someone new?"

Bernie shot me a glare, and I moved to zip my lips.

"That was Constance. She's a bureaucrat and loves to meddle. I'm glad she chose tonight to step in. I suppose that means I need to thank her."

I giggled and pressed my lips shut to stop, but I couldn't help myself. Laughs poured out of me, bringing light into my soul.

"What is so funny?"

"You missed a great opportunity to say bureau-cat. Sorry."

His whiskers quirked as he looked at me.

"Funny. Anyway, she's in charge of handing out assignments. When our charges age and pass to the other side, or we're no longer needed, we are assigned to new people. Millie, my cousin, must be devastated. She loved her charge. I'm convinced she shared our secret about talking, but I'd never rat her out."

The happiness zipping through me popped like a balloon, and I put my hand on his head.

"Wait. What do you mean, no longer needed? Could we be separated? Bernie, I will always need you. I can't lose you," I said, tears falling down my cheeks.

He bumped his head into my hand and let out a loud purr.

"We're going to be together for a very long time. I can't read the future, but I'm not going anywhere. You're a special case, Brynn."

I hiccupped and dashed the tears off my cheeks.

"Don't scare me like that. What do you mean, special?"

"You and your questions," Bernie said, looking over his shoulder as Zane walked into the room. "Some of us get assigned people with abilities. Like you. It's a little different in those cases. Typically, it's a lifelong assignment. Most people assume that people just get a new cat who looks remarkably like the old one, and it's rarely noticed."

"That doesn't mean I have to call you Bernie Two in a few years, does it? I mean, you are getting up there. I don't think I could get used to calling you that."

His green eyes went to slits.

"That makes two of us. We age at a different pace. I won't say we're immortal, but we are extremely long-lived."

I inhaled the sweet smell of the sage as Zane walked past. His face was intent as he carefully went through the room.

"Well, that's a relief. Can I meet Millie?"

"You never know what will happen, Brynn. It's possible. I haven't seen her in decades."

"So, how old are you?" I asked, cocking my head to the side. "You've been with me for over twenty-five years, so..."

"And that's enough Q and A for me," Bernie said, hopping off the table and stalking off. "I'm going to bed. I encourage you to do the same before you fall asleep sitting up."

"Wait! There's still more I want to know!"

His only answer was his hind end as he strode off toward the bedroom, tail waving gently.

"Did you find out what you wanted to know?" Zane asked as he held up the smoking bundle. "And how do I put this out?"

"That's a good question. Maybe run it under water? Or no, then we can't use it again."

"I know. I'll try to put it out like a cigarette. What should I use?"

I dragged myself to my feet, wavering a little as I stood. Bernie wasn't kidding. I needed to go to bed.

"Let's use a saucer."

I grabbed one from the cupboard and watched as Zane carefully extinguished the sage. The smoke was gone, but the smell remained, wreathing us in its embrace.

"I'll keep it in the sink, just in case," he said, wiping his hands. "Ready for bed?"

"I am. I'll tell you about Bernie in the morning. You'll never believe it."

"You'd be surprised at my belief capacity. Thanks to you, it's grown by leaps and bounds."

He kissed me softly on the lips and took my hand, leading me out of the kitchen. My phone picked that moment to chime, letting me know I had a text.

"Hang on," I said, looking at my watch. "If I'm getting a text this late, it might be important."

I dug my phone out of my bag on the counter and frowned as I saw the text from Logan on the screen.

"Couldn't sleep, so I started working on the little house in Coppertown. You'll never guess what I found in the attic."

Zane gently put his hand over the phone and took it from me, sliding it back into my bag.

"Whatever it is, it can wait until tomorrow. You need sleep."

"But..."

"Tomorrow."

I snorted as he took my hand again and led me back to the bedroom. I yawned and tripped over my feet as I walked to my side of the bed. Maybe he had a point.

I stumbled my way into my jammies and slid under the cool sheets, working my feet around Bernie's spot on the bed. He grumbled a little before pressing into my leg and letting out a raspy purr. I settled my head onto my pillow and looked over at Zane.

"Thank you. For everything."

He kissed the end of my nose and bumped our foreheads together.

"Thank you. Once again, you saved the day. Get some rest."

I snuggled into his side and closed my eyes. For once, I didn't see the eyes with flames. I refused to let my mind dwell on Logan. Whatever my cousin had gotten himself into could wait until tomorrow. No matter what it was, our team would handle it. Together. I breathed a quick sigh of relief before sliding into blissful sleep.

DON'T MISS THE JINN IN THE JOISTS!

Something is wrong with Logan Sullivan, and Brynn is determined to help her cousin, whether he likes it or not. When Logan discovers an artifact in the attic of a house they're renovating, everything starts to go sideways.

He unleashes something terrifying, and he's in way over his head. The stakes have never been higher and it's going to be all hands on deck to save Logan and his upcoming marriage.

Join Brynn and Bernie, the wonder cat, as they race to undo the damage before it's too late!

Get your copy in the Summer of 2023!

NEVER MISS A NEW RELEASE!

Thank you for taking the time to read this novel. If you enjoyed the book, please take a few minutes to leave a review. As an independent author, I appreciate the help!

If you'd like to be first in line to hear about new books as they are released, don't forget to sign up for my newsletter. Click here to sign up! https://bit.ly/2H8BSef

BOOKS BY COURTNEY MCFARLIN

A Razzy Cat Cozy Mystery Series

The Body in the Park

The Trouble at City Hall

The Crime at the Lake

The Thief in the Night

The Mess at the Banquet

The Girl Who Disappeared

Tails by the Fireplace

The Love That Was Lost

The Problem at the Picnic

The Chaos at the Campground

The Crisis at the Wedding

The Murder on the Mountain

The Reunion on the Farm

The Mishap at the Meeting

The Bones on the Trail

The Dispute at the Fair

The Commotion at the Race

The Spy in the Sand - Coming in Spring 2025

A Soul Seeker Cozy Mystery

The Apparition in the Attic

The Banshee in the Bathroom

The Creature in the Cabin

The ABCs of Seeing Ghosts

The Demon in the Den

The Ether in the Entryway

The Fright in the Family Room

The Ghoul in the Garage

The Haunting in the Hallway

The Imp at the Ice Rink

The Jinn in the Joists

The Kelpie in the Kennel

The Lady in the Library

The Manifestation in the Mansion - Coming in Spring 2025

The Clowder Cats Cozy Mystery Series

Resorting to Murder

A Slippery Slope

A Mountain of Mischief

Pushing Up Daisies

A Taste of Trouble - Coming Spring of 2025!

Millie the Miracle Cat Cozy Mystery Series

A New Beginning

Stacked Against Us

Volumes of Lies

The Poison Pen - Early Summer 2025

NEW! Finn and Briar Cozy Mystery Series

A Guide to Solving a Murder

A Guide to Uncovering A Secret

A Siren's Song Paranormal Cozy Mystery Series

The Wrong Note

A Major Case

The Missing Beat

Escape from Reality Cozy Mystery Series

Escape from Danger

Escape from the Past

Escape from Hiding

A LITTLE ABOUT ME

Courtney McFarlin currently lives in the Black Hills of South Dakota with her fiancé and their two cats.

Find out more about her books at:
   www.booksbycourtney.com

Follow Courtney on Social Media:

https://twitter.com/booksbycourtney

https://www.instagram.com/courtneymcfarlin/

https://www.facebook.com/booksbycourtneym

A NEW SERIES! MILLIE THE MIRACLE CAT COZY MYSTERY SERIES

Olivia Sutton just moved to Timber Falls, a little town hidden in the mountains of Colorado, with the goal of starting fresh and leaving

A NEW SERIES! MILLIE THE MIRACLE CAT COZY MYSTERY SERIES

her past firmly in the rearview mirror. She's got a plan and some hard-earned savings. How hard could starting over be?

While she's scouting locations to start a new bookstore, she discovers a bedraggled stray cat, and something far more sinister.

Will the people in her newly claimed hometown believe she's innocent? Is she losing her grip on reality or is her new cat capable of strange things?

Join Olivia and Millie the Cat as they work together to save Olivia's reputation, find a killer, and begin living their new lives.

Order Your Copy Now!

HAVE YOU READ THE RAZZY CAT COZY MYSTERY SERIES?

The Body in the Park
A Razzy Cat Cozy Mystery

"I'm a cat lover and read many cat mysteries. Courtney McFarlin's Razzy Cat Cozy Mystery Series is my favorite."

She's found an unlikely consultant to help solve the crime. But this speaking pet might just prove purr-fect...

Hannah Murphy yearns for a real news story. But after a strange migraine results in an unexpected ability to talk to her cat, she must keep the kitty-communication skills a secret if she wants to advance from fluff pieces to covering felonies. And when she literally trips over a slain body, she's shocked her feline companion is the best partner to crack the case.

Convinced she's finally got her big break, Hannah quickly runs afoul of a handsome detective and his poor opinion of interfering reporters. And when she discovers the victim's penchant for embezzlement and fraud, she may need more than a furry friend and a cantankerous cop to avoid ending up in the obits.

HAVE YOU READ THE RAZZY CAT COZY MYSTERY SERIES?

Can Hannah catch a killer before her career and her life are dead and buried?

The Body in the Park is the delightful first book in the Razzy Cat cozy mystery series. If you like clever sleuths, light banter, and talking animals, then you'll love Courtney McFarlin's hilarious whodunit.

More reader comments: "The Razzy Cat series is a joy to read! I have read the first three, and just bought the fourth. These books are well written, engaging stories. I love the positive and supportive relationships depicted amongst the main characters and the cats. That is so refreshing to read. I look forward to more books in this series. I will also be reading some this author's other works. Well done, and keep writing!" - Ingrid

Buy *The Body in the Park* for the long arm of the paw today!

Keep reading for a sneak peek at Chapter One.

BONUS: CHAPTER ONE OF THE BODY IN THE PARK

Friday, June 19th

The hum of the newsroom refused to fade into the background as I worked to file my last story for the day. I'd been assigned a fluff piece, which I usually hated, but considering it was almost the weekend, I wouldn't complain too much. I was looking forward to two blissful days off and some quality time away from work.

I've been working at the paper here in Golden Hills, Colorado, for two years, ever since I graduated from the local college. I'm originally from a tiny town in South Dakota, and I love living so close to the mountains. I'd discovered a love of hiking while I was in college, and I couldn't imagine leaving to go back home to the family farm. There's nothing wrong with farming; we all gotta eat, but for me, I needed mountains and adventure.

I read through my story one more time, checking for errors and stopping to admire my byline. Hannah Murphy, that's me. Seeing my name in print never got old. I hit enter on my laptop, posting my story to my editor with plenty of time to spare on my deadline. I rummaged around under my desk, looking for my purse. With any luck, I'd be

BONUS: CHAPTER ONE OF THE BODY IN THE PARK

able to slip away a bit early and head home. I poked my head over my cubicle and looked over at the glass office where my editor, Tom Anderson, was banging away on his computer. I stifled a laugh. Tom was old school, from a time when the clerical girls typed everything on typewriters, and he resented being forced to use a computer.

I grabbed my things and headed down three cubicles to where my best friend, Ashley Wilson, worked. Ashley was my roommate in college, and we were both journalism majors. While she lived for the lifestyle pages, I was drawn to hard news and wanted to make a name for myself as a reporter. I wasn't kidding myself. I knew it was a miracle our little newspaper had its doors open still. Most small newspapers had folded years ago, and it was tough for an independent outfit to keep the lights on. But I was hoping with some luck, perseverance, and hard work, I'd be able to move up the ranks to a serious news position.

I tapped on the wall of Ashley's cubicle and flopped into the chair across from her desk.

"Hey, Ash, you about done for the day?"

Her tongue was poking out from between her lips as she focused on her screen, ignoring me. I leaned over to see what was engrossing her and saw she was working on an image in Photoshop. Since we were such a small paper, most of us had to do our design work for our stories, which wasn't always fun.

I watched her as she worked, admiring her long brown hair that was impossibly straight and glossy. My hand went up to my unruly nest of blonde locks, and I gave a rueful smile. No matter how often I tried to straighten my hair, it never turned out as pretty as hers.

We were complete opposites. She was tall, statuesque, and dark, while I was short, thin, and fair. She enjoyed shopping and partying, while I was an outdoors kind of girl. It didn't matter, though. I'd never had a friend as close as her. She gave a little shout and hit save, turning to face me.

"Hey, Hannah, sorry about that. The image didn't want to cooperate."

"No worries, been there, done that. What are your plans for tonight? Are you hanging out with Bill, or was it Will?"

"Will. He was also three guys ago. You gotta keep up, girl!"

"Sorry, are you hanging out with what's-his-face tonight?"

"I was unless you wanted to do something. We need a girl's night out."

"We do, but not tonight. I think I've got a migraine coming on. I'll just go home and hang out with my cat."

Ashley made a sad face and heaved a sigh.

"That's how it starts. You're in your twenties, and you spend a Friday night alone, with just a cat for company. Before I know it, you'll be my crazy cat lady friend who becomes a shut-in and only leaves to buy more cat food."

"Wow, that's a depressing and strangely detailed future look."

"I call them as I see them. I kid, Hannah. You should get out more, though," Ashley said, giving me a look.

"I know, I'm just not a peopley person. I enjoy being outside, not cramped in a loud bar with sweaty people being all, I don't know, sweaty. I like my cat. I like quiet."

"I need to find you a man. I think Will had a brother..."

"Thanks, but no thanks. I don't want to get set up with a cast-off's brother. That would be even sadder than being home alone with my cat. Seriously though, have fun tonight. I expect a play-by-play tomorrow."

Her phone rang, cutting off our conversation. I waved as I grabbed my bag to leave. It looked like the coast was clear, so I headed toward the door, determined to make a break for it. I wasn't lying to Ashley; my head was pounding, and I wanted to get home and change into my jammies.

"Hannah! Wait!"

I groaned when I heard Tom's voice, turning on my heels to head back to his office. I stopped in the doorway.

"Hi, Tom. How was my article? Does it need any edits?"

"It was fine. You self-edit well. That's not why I wanted to talk to you," Tom said, gesturing for me to come in and take a seat.

BONUS: CHAPTER ONE OF THE BODY IN THE PARK

I plopped down in the comfy chair across from his desk.

"What's up?"

The way Tom dressed was as old school as the way he typed. His button-down shirt was turned up at the cuffs, exposing a myriad of ink stains. He had a nice face, utterly at odds with his gruff voice. He scrubbed his bald head and leaned back in his chair. He looked at me closely for a beat.

"Hannah, you've been doing a great job lately. I know fluff pieces aren't what you want to do, and I appreciate that you've been good about working on them. I can tell you put in the effort, even though you don't enjoy the subject."

"Thanks, Tom, that's nice of you to say."

"I'd like to try you out on a few tougher pieces. The next big story that breaks is yours."

"Are you serious? I'd love to try some harder news pieces!"

This was the most exciting thing to happen to me in months. I was finally going to sink my teeth into some meaty stories!

"That and whatever else you can dig up. I know you're young, but I think you deserve a shot."

"Thank you so much. I won't let you down."

"See that you don't."

With that, he waved me off and turned back to his computer, cursing under his breath as he started banging on the keys again.

I floated out of his office, almost forgetting my headache. I got to the parking lot and climbed into my ancient Chevy Blazer. I'd saved up my money back in high school, and it was old back then. It had seen me through college, though, and with any luck, it would get me through until I could make enough money to replace it.

Traffic was picking up as I navigated my way back to my apartment. Golden Hills was growing fast, but I was lucky enough to find a place that backed right onto a huge green space. I had acres and acres of wilderness to explore via the trail that led to the Crimson Corral Park. It wasn't cheap, but it was worth it to have an outdoor space and a killer view.

I trudged up to the top floor, feeling my headache get worse with

BONUS: CHAPTER ONE OF THE BODY IN THE PARK

every step. By the time I made it to my door, I was feeling odd. I walked in and immediately tripped over my cat, Razzy. I'd had her for two years, ever since I got my place. I scooped her up and cuddled her close, apologizing for tripping over her. She was a Ragdoll cat, and I had no idea how a beautiful, purebred cat like her had ended up in an animal shelter.

Her soft fur felt like a rabbit, and her little purrs made me smile. She was a quiet cat who rarely meowed. I put her down and walked to the kitchen, trying to decide what to make for supper. A quick check of the fridge revealed I needed to do some serious grocery shopping. As I stood in front of my cabinets, a wave of nausea and dizziness rushed through my body. I gripped the counter to keep from falling over.

Razzy meowed at me, cocking her head to the side. It was like she could tell something was wrong. I skipped dinner and walked back to my bedroom, holding my head. I changed into my favorite pair of fuzzy pajama pants and a tank top. Maybe if I just lay down for a few minutes, I'd feel better. I collapsed onto the bed, and Razzy jumped up next to me, snuggling close. Closing my eyes, I felt darkness rush toward me.

* * *

"Mama? Mama!"

A small voice pulled me from the darkness. I blinked open my eyes, trying to get my bearings. I felt grass underneath my feet. I looked around and realized I was in a park. My stomach felt hollow as I looked around, trying to figure out why I was outside. I glanced down and saw I was still wearing my fuzzy pants and smiled. This must be a dream. At least, in my dream, I didn't have my headache.

"Mama?"

There was that voice again. I looked through the gloom, trying to see if a child was wandering around. This was a strange dream for sure.

"Mama! There you are."

BONUS: CHAPTER ONE OF THE BODY IN THE PARK

A small figure walked toward me and sat in front of me, looking up into my face. It took me a second to recognize my cat, Razzy, sitting there. Her whiskers bristled in the faint light from the moon.

"Say something, Mama. You're scaring me. Why are you outside?"

I felt my world rock as I realized Razzy was talking to me. Like, really talking. I laughed when I remembered I was dreaming. Geez, this was one crazy dream. I shrugged and went with it.

"Razzy, what are you doing in my dream?"

"Um, I'm pretty sure you're not dreaming. I followed you out of the apartment. You left the door open, which isn't safe, by the way. I tracked you here and kept calling you until I found you. Why didn't you answer me?"

Okay, this was weird. She was talking to me like she was a human, and I could understand everything she was saying. This had to be the winner for my strangest dream ever.

"You were calling for your mama. I figured there was a little kid in my dream who was looking for their mother. I didn't know it was you."

"I always call you that. To me, you are my mama," Razzy said, her eyes rounding with concern. "This is weird, though. I always try to talk to you, but it's like you can't understand me. Why are you suddenly understanding what I say?"

"Must be the dream. I'm sure I'm going to wake up any second and find you cuddled up next to me."

"You're not dreaming, but whatever. Can we go home now? It's getting cold."

Razzy fluffed up her fur and turned to her left, looking at me expectantly. Her tail curled into a question mark as I stood there, staring at her. Well, maybe if I followed her, I'd wake up. I must have had something bad for lunch.

I shrugged and followed her.

"Lead on, Macduff," I said, as I fell in behind her.

"It's actually 'Lay on, Macduff,'" Razzy said with a sniff. "Humans, always misquoting things."

"Wait, you know Shakespeare?"

"I know way more than you might think."

I couldn't help but laugh. I had a talking cat who was also a literary critic in this dream. I needed to write this down when I woke up.

Razzy paused, her tail going stiff and then curling down behind her. Her hackles went up, and she sniffed the air.

"Stop, there's something up ahead."

"Are we going to meet a talking dog next? That would be pretty cool."

I moved past her, ready to get out of this dream and wake up back in my apartment. I took a few more steps and fell over something stretched across the sidewalk. As I felt around to see what I'd tripped over, my hand came in contact with something cold and squishy. With a little shriek, I scooted back. This dream had taken a disturbing turn.

I felt in the pocket of my pajama pants and grabbed my cellphone. Switching on the flashlight app, I held it out in front of me, my hands shaking. I wasn't sure I wanted to see what it illuminated.

There, next to me on the ground, was the body of a man. I placed my fingers on his neck and felt nothing there. Jumping up, I screamed, convinced now was the perfect time for me to wake up. I looked over at Razzy. She walked closer, sat down, and shook her head.

"I told you, you're not dreaming. You should probably call the cops."

Realization flooded through me as I took stock of the situation. My feet were freezing on the cold concrete. I checked my arms and noticed I had goosebumps. I pinched myself and winced when I clearly felt it.

Razzy walked over to my feet and gently bit down on the top of my foot.

"Ouch! Why did you do that?" I asked, rubbing my foot.

"You didn't seem to believe me that you're awake. You were

pinching yourself, so I thought it would help if I pitched in too." She gave what I assumed to be the cat version of a shrug. "Call the cops."

I hesitated for a second before numbly obeying her suggestion and dialing 9-1-1 on my phone.

Get your copy now to read the rest!

Made in the USA
Coppell, TX
20 March 2026

74347403R00097